Drawing Down the Moon

by

A. M. Keen

Published under license from Andrews UK

"He met with the Devill, and cheated him of his booke, wherin were written all the witches names in England, and if he looks on any witch, he can tell by her countenance what she is."

Matthew Hopkins

Execution

A mass of flames roared within the winter's night. People flooded to the centre of their town grasping tools and torches, yelling within an atmosphere thick with anger and aggression. Voices babbled into one roar aimed towards the woman who had been judged and sentenced.

"Kill her!" came cries from within the gathering crowd.

"Kill the witch!"

Through the tools and pitchforks emerged a defenceless, fearful woman, yanked into compliance by a firm grasp of her hair. The town's executioner dragged the woman toward her fate across a solid, frozen ground through the increasing mass of bodies. The woman pulled against him as she attempted to escape, but the giant beneath the black hood paid little attention. Try as desperately as she might, he was simply too powerful to resist. The accused wailed between the bodies of the crowd, her battered legs bruised and bloody from their attacks as she passed through. Men kicked her. Women spat on and clawed her skin. The fading dress she wore began tearing from pressure it simply could not withstand. In the wake of her struggle followed the clergyman of the town. She turned back briefly to him, looking for a final chance from God that she may be spared. "Please father, please help me." The reverend continued his journey, clutching a small bible tightly to his chest.

"And unto you we continue His work in His holy name. We deliver you to the Dark Lord, of whose practice you have openly embraced, so that your soul may now take its rightful place within the very flames of Hell itself," he responded. The prayer was all but lost within the thunderous crowd amassed around them.

"Heathen!" came a women's scream.

"I am not a witch!" the accused retorted, still protesting her innocence this late in the trial.

4

At the doorway of a small stone house a young woman stood, looking out at the chaos swarming through the town. The candles burning inside her home flickered within a breeze that drifted through the open door. She stood, tense, as the scene played out across the open town square often used for communal activities. Today the happy community would bear witness to another display of human cruelty, all in the name of the Holy Lord and His good work.

"Ellie, go inside," came a gentle voice from behind. Her father pushed past into the chilly night. He was a large man, his face hidden by a dark beard. Ellie stepped aside to allow his large physique past. "This is not for you to see."

"Are they going to kill her?" Ellie asked.

Her father looked over his shoulder at the baying mob. His expression told her everything she needed to know.

The woman accused continued to fight against the executioner. Her legs and midriff ached from the blows bestowed upon her by onetime neighbours and friends. A bald patch on her scalp bled heavily from the struggle. Her nose had been shattered from the violence inflicted during the final journey. The crowds used their fists, their feet and any weapon which they had managed to find against her. At the centre of the square lay a wooden stake, some fifteen feet in length. Its base was hidden by twigs, branches and logs which would serve as fuel for her punishment, the accusation of witchcraft.

Fear surged within her body as she kicked at her tormentor. Her face struck the cobbled ground and snapped backwards as he retaliated, thrusting her down to the floor with ease. Pain screamed across the side of her face. Her nose and mouth streamed blood. The simple dress now tore at the seams. The executioner lurched down and grasped her hair once more, dragging the barley conscious woman on her stomach. As she teetered on the edge of consciousness, a succession of kicks thudded into her torso, breaking ribs. Each strike sent new pain through her body. Each one brought with it a fresh wound from which she was unlikely to recover.

Lying prone on the freezing ground the stake fell upon the accused's back. Her arms yanked behind the wooden shaft and became bound together, so tightly that they turned white. The villager's assisted the executioner to hoist the limp body, allowing more rope to be threaded underneath and around the stake. It was drawn so tight that her chest restricted, and an already broken body struggled to draw even a rasp of a breath.

The accused watched as the terrain beneath her began to move. The crowd cheered: her fate now sealed.

A deep, circular hole excavated for the trial was cleared of debris by community member's intent on helping. The accused woman had no idea that the crowd was parting, allowing a clear passage through to the town square. Many followed, shouting obscenities and detriment until finally arriving at her destination. Men from the crowd helped as they hoisted the stake in the air and placed its base in the ground. It slid in and stood upright as intended. The crowd cheered as she towered above them, bound so tight she remained aloft, defying gravity. Her pale skin glowed within the orange light created by the flames.

Villagers began throwing fuel wood toward her feet. They cheered and gestured as she remained suspended in the night sky. Through blurred eyes a sea of bodies flames, pitchforks, spades and hoes appeared.

The last of the firewood was thrust to the stake, scratching across her legs. Below, a dignitary lifted a hand to silence the crowd. She recognised him as Mayor Randall, the elected leader of the small community. The crowd's shouts turned to murmurs and eventually to silence; a silence broken only by the roaring of the torches.

"Let this be a lesson!" Randall shouted across the flicker of the burning flames. "Let this be a lesson to all who dare to live amongst us and practice the unholy worship of the Dark Lord! We will not tolerate you! No witch, no warlock nor anything otherwise that may set foot within our holy town! This shall be their fate!" A cheer erupted from the townsfolk as he grabbed a torch and turned to face her. "Miss Bunyon, you have been judged guilty of the crime of witchcraft! Your lies and deceit have insulted our good town, and the Lord God Almighty himself! How dare you! How *dare* you! Your infiltration of our peaceful town will not be tolerated! The Dark Lord's minions will watch on in fear! We will not tolerate you, or anyone who practices the Dark Arts. Your crime is witchdraft. Your punishment is death! May you return to the Hell from whence you were spawned, you foul wench!" The flame ignited the branches and the smell of burning wood wafted immediately from the fire. The crowd cheered and yelled as she began a struggle against the growing fire. So vigorously did she fight that the ropes binding her wrists cut into the skin. More torches were tossed onto the fire increasing the intensity of the flames. Smoke emerged and danced away in to the cold sky. Miss Bunyon struggled as the heat crept up from below, screaming as loudly as her broken body would allow, prompting laughs and taunts from the onlookers. The smoke stung her eyes. With blurred vision, she watched the Reverend make the sign of a cross with his right hand, then return to clutch his bible.

The witch screamed as fire caught the tattered dress and began burning her feet. The pain intensified. Her toes and feet burned black and shrivelled as the flames drew larger, spreading up her legs towards the stomach. Her skin blistered. The dress caught fire at her torso, now hiding cracked, charred skin. Clumps of roasted flesh fell from her thighs. She screamed as the searing heat grew hotter and reached her breast, burning what remained of her clothing and the long hair that had fallen on it. Her screams rang out from the roaring flames, so bloodcurdling that some of the townspeople stopped their jeering.

Miss Bunyon, judged and now executed, released one final scream and fell silent.

Through the cheers of the people Mayor Randall turned to the Reverend. "These woods are full of them," he said, gesturing to the dense forestry that surrounded his township. "These witches, ghosts, lycanthropes and other unholy creatures fester like flies around a rotting carcass."

"Maybe this will serve as a lesson to any who may be watching," the Reverend responded.

"Maybe, but maybe we need to go a stage further."

"Why? Have we not already done God's work as he would wish?"

Mayor Randall placed a hand on the Reverend's shoulder. "We have done a fine job serving the Lord and delivering this heathen to the bowels of Hell, but maybe we should send a greater message."

"And what, pray tell, do you have in mind?"

"I sent message to Parliament not a month past to request the assistance of a Witchfinder. A Witchfinder is someone who can cleanse these parts and allow us to live peacefully."

"A Witchfinder?" the vicar replied. Randall noticed the concern within his voice. "Won't that cost our treasury dearly?"

A cheer erupted as the stake finally gave way to the heat of the fire and collapsed into the flames, along with the blackened body of the cremated woman. A mass of embers launched into the air.

"Father, I would rather ensure the safety of our people at a cost to our town than have our people live in fear of those creatures dwelling beyond our eyes in the safety of the trees, wouldn't you so agree?"

Slowly the clergyman nodded. Randall smiled and patted his back. He turned his attention back to the surrounding forest. There had been many reports of a particular witch lurking outside his town and a community of lycanthropes dwelling within the trees. He knew it would cost the community, but losing shillings was more acceptable than losing lives.

"A Witchfinder will hunt anything unholy in these parts and kill them," he explained. "Not only will it save our township the horror of which we have witnessed this night, but it will also provide a greater consequence for those who may consider turning to worship the Dark Arts."

"And if he doesn't?" the Reverend asked.

"Then there is nothing more that we can do."

Fear

The proud church of Elkwood stood overlooking the township to which it served. Situated on a hill on the outskirts of the town, the religious building served as a symbol of hope and sanctuary to any that set foot within its doors.

On this day, the Lord's Day, the townsfolk began their service on a dull, overcast winter's morning. This Sunday was indeed a bitter one, with a thick frost forming on the town's roofs and open areas. Ice had formed where puddles once lay and icicles hung from ledges where water once ran.

Hymns could faintly be heard across the entire town from the farms at its borders and down into the square, where the smouldering remains of the judgemental fire and its victim still crackled occasionally. The fact that the fire had still burned during such a harsh night suggested to the townsfolk that this lady had indeed been in league with the Devil, and these were the embers of flames from Hell as the Dark Lord returned to reclaim her.

The hymn came to an end, and as it did so Reverend Thomas stepped up the small, wooden staircase to address the congregation from his humble pulpit. The church rustled and creaked with the sound of its flock returning to its benches in preparation for the sermon he was about to deliver. Ellie settled back on to her pugh. A cold, uncomfortable breeze circulated inside the building. During the summer she enjoyed the warm breezes dancing about from outside, but winter was another thing altogether. Ellie knew the biting temperature would ensure the Reverend's words were heard and not missed by dozing churchgoers this Sunday.

"These are strange and troubled times we are living in within our peaceful community, and the Lord's protection and love is what we will need to see us through."

Ellie studied this man of the cloth, preaching the Lord's way against the backdrop of a small glass window. He was a man of sixty or more years. The good Lord had deemed it appropriate to deprive his servant of his hair, except for long stringy grey strands that were found around the base of his head and hung unkempt across his shoulders.

"However, these dark days may lead some to believe that He has forgotten us, or chosen to turn His back on our prayers. This is, of course, untrue. The good Lord will never turn His back on the loyal servants of His cause. He is concerned for us, and for our safety, as the recent events befalling our peaceful town are forged by the hands of the Devil himself!"

The church erupted in to chatter. The Reverend's words appeared to be causing alarm. Ellie sat next to her father in silence, watching the rest of her neighbours expressing their concern and anger. She pushed her long, black hair behind her ears and looked to him.

Reverend Thomas raised his hands in the dull light. Ellie noticed the reassuring smile he delivered to bring the congregation to order. "My children, my children," he began, regaining the attention of the audience, "this does not mean He has forsaken us. It means we must, with His blessing, find our own way to fight the battle between good and evil in His name."

A man stood from the bench ahead of Ellie. "How do we fight a witch as strong as the one plaguing our town? Or those filthy lycanthropes which lurk near? And what about the coven of ghosts haunting these trees? How do we combat them?" Ellie caught a glimpse of Mayor Randall, who turned from his privileged seat in front of the pulpit. The angry man continued. "To catch and trial a witch who is young and inexperienced is simple, but how can we destroy the hag living deep within the woods? She is stronger than any witch ever to plague our town!"

Many of the villagers echoed their agreements in one monotonous murmur.

11

Ellie watched as Mayor Randall looked toward the Reverend and rose from his seat. "Settle down. Settle. Now, it is no secret that we are indeed being tormented by she who dwells within the woods. She will also have help from those corrupted within our good town, like Miss Bunyon whom we discovered last evening, as well as the lycanthropes of which you speak."

"You mean there's more?" a voice shouted.

A moment of silence passed inside the church. Ellie expected the worst. "Yes, we believe there are."

The churchgoers erupted in panic and anger. The timber building rocked to its foundations as the churchgoers raged within its confines.

"Settle down!" boomed the voice of the Reverend above the frustration. "There will be no anger in the house of God!"

The anger subdued immediately. The viciousness with which they shouted made Ellie uncomfortable. The Reverend's voice had been authoritative, and in her eyes, welcome.

Her attention returned to Mayor Randall, who adjusted his clothing as though he was beginning a speech. "Now, the good father and I," he stated, gesturing with an open palm towards the Reverend, "have decided that, yes, you are right, all of you. We can deal with simple witches and informants within our town, but as you rightly say, not against the hag nor the lycanthropes from the forest who torment us and our way of life. Therefore I have sent word to London, to request the assistance of a Witchfinder to aid us in these darkest of times." Ellie listened nervously as the mayor explained his actions. "Now, it will cost us a substantial amount of shillings for his services, and due to the breakdown of trade with our surrounding towns and villages, all whom are afraid to travel the routes to our town, we are in dire financial straits. But I believe that once the witch is finally found and executed the routes will once more be re-established and we will be able to return the finances to our commerce chamber, and thus our town will once again thrive."

"And if it doesn't?" came a man's voice from the middle of the gathering.

"It will, my friend," Randall replied, his voice one of confidence. "The best Witchfinder in England and his company operate within our area. He will rid us of that cursed hag and any other who may be in league with her. Meanwhile, I ask you all to remain vigilant. Watch out for any unusual practices by your mothers, daughters, aunts, nieces and grandmothers, even by your neighbours and the men within our town. Report any suspicious activity immediately."

The sermon came to an end with the Lord's Prayer, after which the townsfolk flooded through the oak doors and down to their frozen town to enjoy the remainder of the day. Ellie's father had remained at the church to speak with Mayor Randall, allowing his daughter to wander down the hill and back to town unaccompanied. As Ellie took the short walk home a body jumped from behind a tree forcing a surprised squeal from her. The smiling face of Jack McDonald filled her eyes, and after a moment's shock she returned the smile.

"For you," he said exuberantly, and placed a cluster of snowdrops in her hand. "Before they vanish." Ellie continued her smile. She was shocked that Jack knew snowdrops would vanish at the end of spring. For some strange reason they had sprouted early this year, February to be exact. This lengthy winter was another event that the town blamed on the witches curse they believed she had cast over them. "One day," Jack began as the pair resumed walking side by side, "I will take you for my wife, Ellie."

"Is that right?" One day she would allow it, but he didn't know that.

"One day," he repeated optimistically. "But until that day, this is all I can offer." He pecked her on the cheek and sprinted away down the hill towards the town. "Until we meet again!" he shouted over his shoulder.

"Fool," she said quietly, clenching the snowdrops in her hand.

Nightfall

As night approached slowly over the sleepy township, Mayor Randall arranged a handful of men around the outskirts of the town to settle the nerves of the people. When darkness fell across the land, imagination wandered and fear spread throughout the community. Fear was a potent weapon, and nothing spread amongst the people more quickly.

The charred remains of the previous night's victim had been buried in an unmarked grave somewhere within the woods. The only people in attendance were Randall, Reverend Thomas and the gravediggers. Once it was dumped in the earth Thomas blessed the corpse and splashed holy water on the grave whilst muttering a prayer. The earth began to fall on the white sheet sewn around the body, signifying the end of the witch and a victory in the name of the Lord. On their slow walk back to the town, Randall and Thomas had decided that sentry duty would be the best action to take. With the old hag lurking somewhere within the trees, and a freshly buried witch, they both feared some kind of retaliation or even resurrection.

Eight men, including the town's executioner, hard-working labourers and farmers, volunteered to take the dangerous posts, each for a shilling apiece. As darkness emerged and the cold night set in, they took their flames and tools before pairing off, each posted on the cardinal points.

Beyond a farm to the east stood Stephen Elcombe and Ray McDowell, two men who worked in the town's windmill. Tonight both men guarded the structure in which they worked so laboriously.

"You believe she was a witch?" Elcombe asked as their amber flame illuminated the small area they were guarding. Ray leant against the timber fence that separated the field from the woods, placed his elbows on the top slat and looked in to the trees.

"Certainly," he replied, gently sighing in the darkness. He caught sight of his own breath and suddenly felt just how cold the winter's night had become. "She was an odd one that Miss Bunyon, that was certain. Using plants to heal herself, and using her left hand for everything she did. Aye, she was a witch alright. What more proof do you need? "

Stephen turned to him. "What do you make of the Witchfinder heading to town? You really think that a man can kill a witch? I mean, if the hag decides to use her powers I don't see how anyone can contend with her?"

"Stephen, you forget that a Witchhunter is skilled in all things strange that lurk in these dark lands. He has a team who will be just as experienced. There will be ways to counter her spells that we as commoners are unaware of, but a Witchfinder? He'll know. He's probably seen everything she will throw at him and laugh in her face."

Ray looked to the sky and watched as the full moon passed silently behind drifting clouds. A sharp wind drifted between the trees at the edge of the woods. Darkness smothered the light and engulfed the town, leaving only the flickering flames at the outskirts where the sentries were posted.

Ray returned his gaze in to the darkness. A loud rustle broke the silence. "What was that?" he asked.

"What?"

"Just then. Did you hear it?"

"What?" Stephen asked again.

"There. The trees rustling."

"The trees... Ray, we're on the outskirts of the woods. Of course you're going to hear leaves and branches in the wind."

"No, it sounded like something was there." Stephen turned and looked into the looming darkness. Ray followed his gaze in to the landscape behind the trunks and branches, now illuminated by the flickering, amber torch. He peered into the forest, squinting in an attempt to sharpen his focus.

Stephen looked quickly across. "I don't see or hear anything. Maybe your imagination has got the better of you?"

Ray shot back a glare, annoyed that his comrade did not believe him. "There is something out there," he said bluntly, holding his own torch at arm's length.

"I'll check," Stephen replied.

"Don't-"

"Ray!" Stephen snapped, "I'll just have a quick look."

Ray sighed. "Quickly, then get back. I'm telling you there's something out there."

"I won't be long. You think I want to be out there? No, I don't. If I see or hear anything I'll be right back."

The wind breezed past, ruffling their clothes and breaking the eerie silence. Ray offered nothing in reply but a simple nod.

Stephen turned and left the borders of the town, carrying his flickering light and his pitchfork. Ray watched as his friend vanished beyond the trees.

He waited in the cold, open air, looking up to the treetops that roared with every gust as the breeze became more forceful. The branches swayed against the patchy sky. He looked over towards the town in an attempt to see the torches of the other sentries. There were none. A shiver ran down his spine. A frisson of fear crept over him and he looked back in the direction of the trees. The torchlight Stephen was carrying had been swallowed by the darkness.

Ray began pacing along the fence, waving the torch to see into the night. The trees waved back as the wind became more constant around their branches. The darkness engulfed him. His fear intensified. Stephen was still lost to the forest. He continued pacing, his feet scraping the forest debris as he moved. A howl surged through the trees. The sentries posted around the town, Ray included, stopped and listened as the beastly roar echoed from the forest. It whistled away into the skies and vanished in the darkness. From the distance another howl began, softer and more distant. Ray froze. The final howl echoed as it fell silent, replaced by the sound of the wind in his ears. He stood in front of the threatening trees. The clouds fragmented by the wind as they sailed across the full moon. The flame on Ray's torch flickered as the wind took hold. He held it towards the forest. Somewhere in there Stephen lurked, and Ray was overwhelmed by an uneasy feeling that his friend was not alone. The wind plastered his clothes against him. Finally he drew courage.

"Stephen?" he said nervously in the dark void. "Stephen, are you all right?" Nothing responded but the swaying leaves chattering in the breeze. Still no torch light from the depths of the forest. "Stephen?"

A growl rumbled near to the labourer. His eyes widened. The flame in his grasp offered little light in the blustering wind. He could see nothing. A scream, a roar, and Ray fell heavily to the grass. Dazed momentarily he rolled sideways, placing a hand on his chest which ached. He checked himself for injury and poked his body, sensing he had been harmed. His chest was as it should be and there was no tear to his clothing. He had been struck by something, and struck violently. Adrenalin surged through his veins. Quickly, Ray scampered to his feet and turned to the flame still burning on the ground. Rubbing his chest he stooped down and picked up the light in a clean sweep, spun round immediately and turned to face the forest. Nothing. A patch of blood began to seep from his heavy coat. Fearing the worst he pulled open the garment and tore his buttoned shirt to see the injury. All he could find was skin, stained orange by the feeble light of the flame of his torch, nothing more. After a moment of relief he began scouting the area to see what had knocked him down. Whatever it was had been injured. Nothing left blood behind and remained unhurt. What had hit him? What had left blood? Debris, twigs and rocks were all he could find in the flickering light waved in the darkness. He stepped further on. His heart sank. On the frost lay a severed leg, bleeding profusely from its stump. Blood trickled across the frost. Bone and muscle glistened in the light of the flame. "Good Lord," Ray whispered in to the cold air, his breath steaming as it left his mouth. A roar blasted his ears and he crashed to the floor. A huge weight smashed on top of him, pinning him against the frozen ground. He squirmed and wriggled as he attempted to escape. A muzzle snapped down towards his throat. He smelled the foul breath of his attacker as it bore down upon him. Saliva plastered his face and chest. The beast snarled as he attempted to escape. A vibrant amber eye glared from the darkness. Ray screamed out, hoping someone would hear.

The sentries, holding their weapons and torches, began running in the direction of the cry. The air filled with the rapid thudding of their booted feet as they tore through the town. Concerned residents appeared at their doors.

The men ran in the direction the scream was coming from. Slowly a figure appeared ahead of them, stumbling back through the darkness. The men slowed as Ray entered the torchlight, his face gashed and bloodied. The shredded hands he used to fend off the beast clutched his throat. Skin flapped from a torn eyelid. He panicked and moved erratically whilst struggling for breath. Mayor Randall emerged from the middle of the group of men along with Reverend Thomas. Ray's eyes welled with tears and he began to sob. Slowly his hands lowered. The throat had been torn away. Shards of skin dangled and flapped as he collapsed in front of the onlookers. Crimson muscle and ligaments protruded from the opening.

"My God..." Randall whispered.

Ray grunted and groaned through his tears. "Wolf..." he croaked before falling to the road. Behind him in the distance two eyes pierced the darkness.

"LYCANTHROPE!" Thomas screamed.

The wolf roared and sprinted toward them. The onlookers dispersed and began running in different directions. "RUN!" came a shout from within the rabble. Tools clattered to the ground. The wolf bounded over the fallen body of Ray and charged toward the fleeing

18

bodies. Thomas clutched the Bible to his chest. Men bounded past in a mad stampede. The lycanthrope swiped the legs of a farmer at the back of the group. He tumbled to the ground as his shins severed in half by the beast's claw. Thomas turned back and focused on sprinting. The mob ran in to the town square, leading the wolf where they had not intended. It pounced on a labourer beside Reverend Thomas, knocking both to the floor. Thomas flew through the air, crashing to the ground a way away from the strike. The wolf roared and clamped its jaws down on the neck of its victim. Thomas watched as the beast ravaged the victim. Its jaw tightened around the neck and crushed, its fangs sliced through the flesh, severing the head between its teeth. The wolf shook its muzzle and launched the decapitated limb in to the air. The town erupted in chaos. Women screamed. Men dashed for safety. Torches littered the floor like small camp fires. Discarded tools lay about the square. The huge wolf looked around at the chaos. Reverend Thomas rolled slowly away. The lycanthrope turned its attention toward the fallen clergyman. Its snout dropped slowly and its eyes squinted. The ground trembled with the deep rumble echoing from its chest.

Thomas began shuffling across the ground on his back, his eyes fixed on the creature.

"Our Father, who art in heaven," he began, too afraid to stand and run. He continued pushing himself away. The lycanthrope moved from the fallen body of its victim and began stalking the servant of God. "Hallowed be thy name, thy kingdom come, thy will be done…." The prayer offered nothing but comfort. The wolf continued to stalk. Slowly it drew upon Thomas. He was gripped by fear and finally stopped moving. He stopped praying and looked into the eyes of his tormentor. It snarled and revealed huge, sharp teeth. "Dear God!" Thomas blurted. The lycanthrope opened its mouth and roared.

A whistle sliced through the air. Blood explode across Thomas' face. The beast lurched and thudded to the ground beside him, howling and screeching as it writhed on the frost. Thomas turned as it

19

began to lurch and twitch in a seizure. Hair began to fall from its body, revealing grey skin. Bones cracked. They broke and contorted as the shape of the wolf turned to that of a human. The full form of a naked man lay beside the Reverend where the wolf had once existed. He lay covered in sweat, releasing steam into the cold air. From its side a silver arrowhead emerged from between the ribs. Reverend Thomas lay upon the frost and looked up at the sky. An overwhelming surge of relief overcame him as he looked toward the clouds. He turned back to the fallen lycanthrope. "The Devil's work," he whispered, of that he was sure.

From across the square a crossbow had been pulled. Five men stood illuminated by their lanterns. All were pilgrims, clad in felt hats and thick capes, sheltering them from the seasonal elements. The shooter of the arrow replaced the crossbow over his shoulder and drew up his cape. The man at the head of the group looked around at the stunned townsfolk staring at them. "I'm looking for Mayor Randall," he shouted, in a nasal voice.

"That would be me," Randall replied, raising a nervous hand in the air. The pilgrims slowly led their horses to the mayor. A group of people made their way across to Reverend Thomas and helped him to his feet. "It seems we arrived at exactly the right time," the pilgrim added, smiling from beneath the rim of his hat. "I believe you sent for me? My name is Hopkins. Matthew Hopkins."

Witchfinder General

An overcast dawn broke across Elkwood. Flames flickered and died, leaving the townsfolk with only the illumination of a huge fire burning in the middle of the square. Few of them had slept much after the attack on their town, and many gathered together, talking, musing, and fearing the attack launched upon them during the dark hours. Many of the women looked alike, with coifs covering their hair and petticoats hidden by aprons. Those men with status in the community wore different coloured linen shirts to demonstrate their position. Mayor Randall and Reverend Thomas were never seen out of their black coloured garments, which demonstrated their respectability to those whom they served. Children were often found wearing shades of blue, as were the servants who tended the mayor in his home. Most of the men wore shades of russet and pale brown, the colour that signified their role within the countryside.

For the first time, the people of Elkwood were afraid. The fear was palpable even as they tended their daily chores. People spoke, as they often will. Talk of the Devil was on most lips. Even the arrival of Matthew Hopkins and his company of hunters did nothing to settle their nerves.

The body of the lycanthrope burned within a fire, in almost the same position as the witch, not two days before. Two graves had been excavated in the churchyard for the sentries who had perished the previous evening. Ray McDowell had succumbed to his wounds almost instantly, but the farmer who had lost his limbs in the lycanthrope attack had hung on for a while longer until the severity of his injury took him away. Stephen Elcombe had not returned from his investigation in the forest, and the people had widely assumed that the decapitated leg they had found belonged to him.

Fear crept across the town as rapidly as the miserable dawn, and Mayor Randall felt it in the air as he wandered across the frozen ground, past the fire. His townspeople watched in groups as he strolled with the Witchfinder by his side. The heat from the fire was warm and welcoming on this early, bitter dawn. Farmers continued tending their livestock but kept a watchful eye on their new visitor as he ambled beside their leader. Behind the Mayor and his guest, another from Hopkins' company followed closely with a crossbow strapped across his back. His body was more exposed than his counterparts, with only a white linen shirt and dark leather waistcoat protecting his torso from the elements.

"It would seem you have more than just a witch to contend with out here," Hopkins stated as they took their walk.

"Indeed we do," replied Randall, pushing his long, grey hair behind his ears. "We knew the lycanthropes existed in the forest and have survived such attacks before. I've always believed us able to protect ourselves."

"I'm sorry to say that it didn't seem so last night."

They wandered in silence. Frost crunched beneath their footsteps. Randall noticed Hopkins and his follower had the luxury of sturdy boots for their long, gruelling journeys. Many of the townsfolk, the Mayor included, wore nothing but simple, leather footwear.

"No, it did not appear that way at all," he responded, a moment or so later.

"Well," Hopkins began, slapping the Mayor on his back and revealing a warm smile, "you did the right thing sending for us. I have a group of men experienced in all aspects of the occult and unworldly. Daniel here, for instance, is an accomplished lycanthrope hunter."

Randall looked over his shoulder at the archer. The young man tipped his hat.

"A little young, wouldn't you say?" he whispered to Hopkins as he turned back.

The Witchfinder leant in and whispered. "Skills can bless anyone, no matter what their age or faith. The twenty-five year old behind you has hunted almost all lycanthropes in the British Isles to extinction. It was he who discovered their allergy to silver. Did you know that when a lycanthrope is in human form it can be destroyed the same as you or I? But, if the lycanthrope has taken the wild form of a wolf, it may only be destroyed by a weapon forged of pure silver?"

"No. No, I did not," Randall replied, somewhat troubled by this information. His general belief, and that of his people, had always been that a lycanthrope could be slaughtered in much the same way as any other animal roaming the forest.

The three men wandered to the square where the wolf burned. The heat rose in a shimmering haze from the flames. To their right a pig pen stretched from the boundary of a simple house. Its three occupants grunted loudly as they foraged for food hidden in the frozen mud. Behind, the forest stretched out across the miles.

"Keep looking ahead," Hopkins ordered.

"What?" Randall asked.

"Just keep looking as though we are talking. Daniel, do you see?"

"Ah – huh," the archer grunted.

"How many?"

"Just the one, sir."

"What?" Randall barked, frustrated.

"Behind the pen," Hopkins began.

Randall turned his head.

"Don't look!" Hopkins snapped in a whisper, "you'll alert it to our awareness."

"Un-noticed," Daniel reported, "still there."

"What is?"

"Tell him, Daniel."

"A young lady with shoulder-length, red hair. Hiding in the shrubbery behind the pen. She's watching the fire. Very tearful. Pale skin, dirty clothing. It suggests she is living in the forest."

23

"Exactly," Hopkins agreed.

"She is looking at the fire where the body is burning. The body is a man. Her reaction suggests this may have been her spouse."

Randall pieced it together. "Then she must be-"

"One of them," Hopkins interrupted.

The three men stood in the cold dawn chill, their skin warming from the fire burning across the way. "Now they know," he added, "and they'll be back."

***

Ellie stood looking out at the cold morning from the doorway of her home. The fire had been burning since dawn and had dwindled now to glowing embers. She had been uncomfortable with the burning of the lycanthrope but enjoyed the warmth that had resulted from its cremation. The houses that surrounded the square had been closed and locked, or so she had believed. The arrival of the Witchfinder had sent unease throughout the townspeople. Many of them were superstitious. They spoke about the lycanthropes and also of witches and ghosts lurking within the woods around them. They spoke of vampires existing in lands afar, and the bodies of the dead rising from their graves in places even further beyond. She had always chosen not to believe stories she could not vouch for, but now, having seen it with her own eyes, she accepted fully that lycanthropes were not confined to the imagination. Before, she had been so afraid of the stories that had been whispered around Elkwood that she chose to dismiss them in an attempt to assuage her own fears and anxieties.

She returned to her bed, closing the door behind her. Her father had started logging early that morning and she had already prepared everything she had needed to cook a meal ready for his return. She had been feeling unwell for some time. Physically, she was well. But her mind, well, that was different. She had been troubled by terrible dreams, so vivid and frightening that they had terrified her from the

24

very start. Visions of a dead mother returning to their home haunted her sleep. Shadows of people long past hovered, floating gracefully between the flames of the burning town. The thing that upset Ellie most was the vividness with which her mind created them. The dreams felt real. The one occurring vision that constantly revisited was the image of her mother. Her long, linen dress appeared dirty and torn, her fingers long and eerie. Lifeless eyes pierced the orange haze of the burning buildings from which she appeared. Her hair waved as though floating in water. Yet through all the fear that engulfed Ellie, there was also the sense of love and affection that the strange apparition brought with her. Often, her mother would be reassuring, foretelling the worst but explaining that whatever doesn't kill you, makes you stronger. The phantom always explained to Ellie she would change forever, and change for the worse.

As Ellie lay on her crumpled blankets she felt the heaviness of sleep bear down upon her. She began to relax, and drifted closer to unconsciousness. The sounds of the town outside faded until finally she drifted quietly away.

Ellie awoke a little while later, immediately sensing something wrong. Launching herself from bed she flew down the stairs. Ellie made her way to the door. An intense heat surged between gaps around the frame. Without any consideration she clattered outside in to the burning town. The sky glowed orange as fire reached upwards, consuming the buildings. Charred bodies of the townsfolk burned on the square. People ran past, screaming, their bodies on fire. The air filled with agony. Ellie was petrified. Her heart pounded. The town immersed in a sea of cries and screams. A fire roared within the centre of the square. Ghosts dragged struggling townsfolk across the blood-stained ground to its flames. They fought. They kicked. They screamed, to no avail. All demised within the flames. Ahead of the fire a woman appeared that Ellie recognised. She became drawn to the figure. Ellie continued her approach, walking barefoot across the terrain. A breeze plastering her gown against her body. She walked,

25

palms turned outward at her hips, almost embracing the surrounding chaos. Dying people staggered, their blackened skin glowing orange within the cracks of their burnt skin. Though petrified, her will forced her onward. She stepped across bodies of the fallen, drawn to the woman who faced the fire. She could see her long, dark hair floating mid-air. As she approached the woman turned, her face twisted to a look of malevolence.

"Ellie," she beckoned, reaching outward. "Ellie, my love." Emotion swept throughout the madness. Ellie took her mother's hand. They gazed on one another as Hell erupted from the flames around them, their hands bonded together in blood. "It is time," her mother began as they turned to the bright, burning fire. "They will come for you."

Ellie stood transfixed by the flames. Her mind understood what the phantom said, but expression registered no surprise or distress at what had been revealed.

"Who will?" she asked softly.

"All of them. The town will judge you."

"Why? Why do I need to be judged?"

"The people fear what they cannot explain, and you will be feared. Do not be afraid. No matter what happens, remember you will rise again."

"From what?"

Mother turned to daughter, revealing eyes with no pupils. "From death."

The ground trembled. Ellie awoke from the trance she had fallen. The air filled with thunder. The buildings shook. The quake drew stronger. The town shook. Ellie lost her balance and released her mother's hand. "Remember Ellie! Be strong! Do not fear!"

The church upon the hillside cracked. The spire swayed. The house of God trembled and split, engulfing the town with the roar of its collapse. It smashed to the floor sending mortar and debris high into the sky. Buildings collapsed. Ellie swayed from side to side as she ran, stumbling beyond people who screamed and reached out to her. She ran with no direction. Across the square, outside Mayor Randall's home, Ellie came to a standstill. It was about to collapse. Turning away Ellie found she had been surrounded by hundreds of shadows, all of them blocking her escape. The ghosts peered lifelessly back to her. "No!" she shouted as the house crashed down around her. "NO!"

"Ellie!" came a scream. It came from the real world. She awoke to a violent earthquake shaking the home. Pots echoed and glass smashed. The house shook with the ferocity of the tremor. Ellie screamed. The quake intensified and quaked stronger. The timbers swayed. Dust tumbled from the crevices. She grasped blankets to her chin, hiding her mouth and catching her tears. The quake subsided. Objects clattered to a standstill. Ellie panted as she gazed about the room. Cracks appeared in the walls. Supporting timbers had buckled. Her brow drenched with sweat, her breathing shallow and rapid.

The bedroom door flung open. Her father glared wildly, his fear and apprehension apparent.

Lore

Night drew across the town and brought with it a dense fog which crept silently from the forest. Slowly it drifted from the darkened depths and swirled across the town, hiding the branches of all but the closest trees. Clusters of twigs poked out like bodiless limbs, a sign that no matter how much was hidden a world still existed beyond the town's borders. The simple buildings loomed from their place as the element swirled along the deserted streets. Amber glows flickered from the windows of the houses as candles illuminated the winter darkness. The sound of cattle upon the town's outskirts drifted invisibly through the darkness. Every building in Elkwood stood tight against the next, forming small alleys and cut-throughs which the townspeople stumbled between at this late hour. Sound from a neighbouring household were very clear to the people living inside, and the sounds from outside, although loud and sometimes excessive, became manageable and part of life to all who lived there. Only the buildings on the town's square received any peace, partly due to its position on the Elkwood boarder, but partly due to fear and ramifications from disturbing the town's Mayor. This night, though, this dark and foggy night, fear had finally taken the town's residents. Those who did not choose to drink within the large tavern locked themselves behind doors and kept the darkness out.

Mayor Randall's open lounge contained large, luxurious chairs which he used to conduct meetings of the township. An immense fire roared in a stone fireplace, repelling the cold air that penetrated the nooks from outside. Tonight's meeting was neither political nor cultural. Tonight he was joined by Reverend Thomas, Andrew Mian, the Secretary of Commerce, and the Witchfinder General Matthew Hopkins.

A maid entered bearing warm drinks. She placed the tray on a small table in the middle of the meeting area and left silently, closing the double doors behind her. Hopkins had been watching out of the window towards the edges of the town. A small light burning from the church glimmered through the fog. After a moment the Witchfinder joined the meeting, sitting in an armchair. Randall made small talk as he handed out the drinks. Hopkins thanked him and took a sip of the tea.

"Now," the Witchfinder began, as he laid the cup back on the table, "tell me everything."

The dignitaries looked at one another.

"First," Mian began, leaning his slight body in the chair, "you explain to us what your experience is, and why it will cost us so much for the privilege."

Hopkins noticed Mian's hostility and forced a smile.

"Master Mian, I take it you know nothing of my reputation?"

"This is a small, self-sufficient community Master Hopkins, the world tends to pass us by un-noticed. Do not be offended by my ignorance."

"Of course not Master Mian, of course not." The smile vanished from Hopkins' face and was replaced with a sinister look from beneath his moustache and beard. "I am appointed by the highest authority within Parliament to hunt down and execute witches who terrorise the towns and villages of our grand country. They plague our counties, gentlemen, and thrive on the fear of the people they live amongst. Usually I do not take work within the fine county of Northamptonshire, I will admit, but considering the severity of your problem as explained in your letter, and having witnessed with my own eyes the lycanthropes that torment your forest, I am happy to vacate my usual haunts within Essex to assist you. You are all in grave danger and I will do my utmost to help and to serve your community and your town."

"And what of your company? I expected you to be travelling only three strong, and with members of the fairer sex." Randall asked. Hopkins mused at the Mayor's research. Not many towns knew this.

"My good man, you are indeed correct. Usually that is how I journey, but due to the severity of your situation I decided it best to bring more men and, hence, more experience. The problems which plague your town are greater than anywhere I have served in England. Now, if you will, please brief me on this most dreadful of situations so I may begin my preparations."

"There is much to tell," Father Thomas began, resting a copy of the Holy Bible firmly upon his lap.

"Then it best to start at the very beginning."

The fog rolled in thickly as the meeting drew onward. Hopkins' men were across town, some making merry in the tavern they were staying. The Witchfinder imagined various flickers of candlelight faded from the town's houses as the fog became thicker, and wooden beams supporting the first floors stretched out into the gloomy light. Almost every town where he had trialled the persecutors of evil acted in the same way. Human instinct was incredibly similar in this day and age. Few people would walk the small streets. Fear had truly taken hold of Elkwood, a scenario he was all too familiar with.

"Many years ago, we expelled a witch from this town when her practice in the dark arts came to our attention," Thomas began, placing his own cup down beside that of Hopkins on the small table. "We knew nothing of the trials such as we deliver today, and I admit we should have returned her to the Dark Lord himself."

Hopkins expressed no sign of judgement at the Reverend's admission.

"Our crops didn't grow, our people were struck down with a fever and many now rest within the grounds of our church."

"Hardly proof of a witches work," he retorted.

"None," Mian added quickly, "but take in to consideration her tending of the sick with herbs, vegetation, magical brews, and you must see our concern?"

"Of course." Hopkins nodded his head gently.

The Reverend took a sip of his tea. "We decided it best to expel her from our town in an act we thought would keep us safe from her effects."

Mian interrupted in with the facts. "We encouraged the people to stone her when she refused to leave."

Hopkins noticed a look of dejection or dismay cross the clergyman's face, who met his gaze with woeful eyes. "And finally she did leave, bloodied, battered and bruised, vanishing somewhere in to the surrounding forest. At that time we knew nothing of the standards of trialling and deemed this appropriate."

Hopkins considered their actions during a pause. Mayor Randall was the one to finally break the silence. "But it wasn't. As the good Father states, our crops withered and died. Many of our people succumbed to a strange fever that swept throughout the town. People started talking of the witch's curse, and soon our situation was common knowledge in the surrounding towns and villages with which we traded."

"Traders heading to or leaving this town would vanish without a trace. Their money and goods would remain untouched along with their horses and cart, but they themselves would disappear, nowhere to be found and are still unheard of, even to this day," Mian explained. "Surely, if the trader was to run away he would at least take his money and horse, but everything was left on the road. Everything, except the person himself."

Randall leaned closer to the Witchfinder. "And as word passed around, many people and towns refused to trade with us, through fear of the witch plaguing our community. To this day we rely solely on ourselves to keep our town fuelled and fed."

A silence filled the room as Hopkins deliberated the situation. The only sound came from the flicker and crack of flames burning from the fireplace.

"I can assure you I will help your town, Master Randall, and I will not leave until this curse is lifted," Hopkins stated with confidence. He looked at each man in turn. "I will help you, and I will rid the curse hanging above your township and good people."

"And for that, Master Hopkins, we thank you." Hopkins noted the Mayor's demeanour. It seemed a huge weight had been lifted from him.

"Now, tell me about this hag that dwells within the forest. The one you believe the cause of this outrage."

Randall grabbed his cup and took a mouthful of tea. "We know very little," he said as he placed it back on the table. Hopkins watched as the Mayor stood and wandered to the fireplace, resting his elbow upon the mantle. "She lived on the outskirts of the town. No one ever saw her walking these streets. She never attended our church, never spoke to anyone. She was a hermit, if you will."

"May I enquire as to a name for this wench?"

"A very, very long time ago she went by the name of Margaret Addler. We grew up together during our early years, both being a similar age," Reverend Thomas explained, appearing more knowledgeable on the subject than his superior. "As Margaret grew older she became more and more corrupted by the dark arts, until the people no longer used her given name. She was referred to as Luna, because of her worship of the night. As the years drew on the toll of her practice became apparent and her appearance grew haggard, then grotesque. By that time she had withdrawn from society and lived alone on the outskirts of our community."

"A recluse," Hopkins mused, leaning back in his chair. His elbows rested upon the arms and a finger supported the side of his face. "Any animals noted within her vicinity?"

"Animals?" Mian repeated.

"Yes, Master Mian. Recluses often use various animals to spy within their townships."

"How do they do that?"

"Master Mian, how is of no importance at this precise moment. I must simply find out if any have been seen in or around her home before she was expelled!"

"None to my knowledge," Reverend Thomas said quickly, "she was alone whenever she was observed."

Hopkins grunted in acknowledgement. "And others? Did she infect any of your people with the Devil's work?"

Randall snorted. "A few," he began, taking the cup from the mantle. "Women, well, girls really."

"She got to them soon after her expulsion. Corrupted their young minds," Thomas continued. Hopkins was drawn to the manner in which he clutched the bible. The Reverend's demeanour, his nervousness, this man was most certainly afraid. "We felt terrible about their execution."

Hopkins leant forward and comforted the priest by placing a hand on his knee. "Father, when the Devil is at work you must act swiftly. You did so, and you did correctly. The young are usually targets for witches, and hags are very persuasive with their strong minds and powerful influence. Tell me," he said, addressing all of the dignitaries, "how did you trial the accused?"

"By taking statements from our townsfolk," Mian informed him. "We acted upon their accusations."

"Indeed. People care for their town and will always report anything beyond the ordinary. There are many different ways to trial an accused, but power of the people is often the most trustworthy. Do you have a magistrate?"

Randall shook his head. "I am the upholder of law. We are a small community against the rest of the world I am afraid, and we have never needed the services of one until we became cursed."

"Understandable. Most understandable. And your work within the role has been commendable. What of a physician? Do you employ one within your fine community?"

"Indeed, a Master Nicholson, who practices not one hundred yards away. Usually he is requested to tend working injuries and fevers."

"More recently he has been called upon to confirm the death of those who have been executed," Mian explained.

"Is this physician practised in symptoms of wiccan or paganism?" Hopkins asked as he reached for his drink.

Reverend Thomas placed the bible in his lap. "Alas, no. There is very little knowledge of the subject, at least in Elkwood. We are cut off from civilisation, more so now since our trade has been all but vanquished."

Hopkins smiled. "Of course. You have been wise to trial only those whom you are certain of practising the Dark Arts. Now, where do you believe this cursed hag dwells within the forest?"

Randall appeared thoughtful if only briefly. "We do not know for sure, but we believe she is settled near to a clan of lycanthropes far from our borders."

"Ah yes, the lycanthropes," Hopkins mused. "This could pose a problem."

"Why? Are you unable to assist us now?" Mian asked.

"No, Master Mian, I have the best hunters within my company. We will rid your town of the witch's curse and we will stay until it is safe to leave. I will, however, have to ask for a higher fee for such a dangerous venture."

"A higher fee!" Mian shouted.

"Yes, a higher fee. You will undoubtedly recognise the danger my company places itself within, ridding your town of a witch whilst a clan of lycanthropes roams freely at your borders. In effect we are battling two dark forces, and that must be recognised by you fine gentlemen, by rewarding us appropriately."

"And tell me, Master Hopkins, how much will a company such as yours, with the expertise of which you speak, cost our town, considering the dire situation to which our treasury currently finds itself?"

Mayor Randall raised a hand toward the Secretary of Commerce, likely to halt any further tirade. "Perhaps you should tell us of the expertise your company brings?" he asked.

Hopkins sensed immediately that the dignitaries would not part with any money until certain they had made a wise investment. "Certainly, my good men, certainly. I ride with four others, as you have already seen. Firstly, there is Daniel Wade."

Hopkins had travelled the length and breadth of the country to trial those accused of witchcraft. Many, many hours, days, months and now years he had spent keeping the company of various hunters. But these four men, like himself, were the best in their trade. These four men, two of which he did not trust completely, had trialled with him on most quests. Hopkins knew exactly how each one would act in any situation. Considering the late hour now passing over the town, the Witchfinder knew exactly where each of his company would be and what they were doing.

Hopkins' mind opened and he took a journey, through Elkwood to the tavern, where the young Daniel Wade of whom he would speak, would most certainly be sat in quiet corner, illuminated by a candle flickering on the wall above him. He would be a spectator in the merriment of a companion.

"Daniel is only a man of early adulthood, but proved to have the greatest of eyes when firing his weapon of choice, the crossbow. His family were slaughtered by lycanthropes whilst he was but an infant. His hatred for their kind runs deep. The young man studied the shape-shifters intensely and discovered their allergy to the purest silver when in wolf form. All his weapons, whether bearing blades or munitions, contain this element, and his sharp eye and shooting skills allow him to be far from the field of battle but just as effective as though he be standing by your side. Then, there's John Stearne."

Within the same tavern, sitting a stone's throw away from Daniel, would be John Stearne, at a table pouring liquor down his gullet as fast as he could take it. The ale would seep from the side of the tankard he was drinking and run between the black bristles of his unkempt beard.

"John is a man I do not fully understand. His history in the art of witch hunting goes back through the years, and I have found him to be very persuasive with gaining confessions from the accused. His methods are questionable, but his results are effective."

"And what are his methods?" Mian asked.

"Master Mian, they are brutal, but they are the methods that have revealed even the most camouflaged, seasoned witch. I pray you do not witness them within your fine town. "Then we have Master William Jones, a man of the church such as yourself, Reverend Thomas."

William Jones could certainly be found knelt in prayer at this late hour, most likely toward the foot of the bed in which he was about to sleep. Hopkins knew that his chamber rested above the noisy tavern where it was likely the two of his company were making merry. William had expressed his dismay to Hopkins earlier. Staying in this small room stood against his moral principles. He detested to even set foot within a building awash with ale and drunkards. On realising there was nowhere else available to stay, he had given in, and would now be repenting his sins to accept this resting place. A man of older years, maybe ten or so more than Hopkins, his grey hair was short but scruffy and his face bore the wrinkles of the Lord's concerns over the fifty years he had walked the earth. Hopkins visualised his comrade, eyes closed, hands clasped together in prayer, ears oblivious to the ruckus below.

"Reverend Jones attends with us to see the good Lord's work done as He would wish," Hopkins began, moving forward, clasping hands and resting his elbows on his knees. It had always been a comfort to those whom Hopkins served, to know that his company and their practices were overseen by a religious man. "Now, Reverend Jones has experience in the realms of exorcism, demons, and souls of the departed."

"Ghosts?" Thomas asked.

"Yes, Father. As a man of experience I know how dangerous ghosts can be. They are everywhere, in all townships and villages, usually loitering around the accused or other devils' spawn."

"From time to time we have been haunted by the spirits of a coven, long since departed."

"Witches?" Hopkins asked.

"Yes, Master Hopkins. We do not believe they were part of this township, rather that they haunt the forest in its entirety."

"Father, you have my word that should we encounter these spirits, Reverend Jones will be more than capable of dispelling them."

"Lycanthropes?" Randall asked from across the room. "Can you deal with their kind?"

"We can deal with anything un-human," Hopkins informed the Mayor, his eyes squinting as though in warning. "Reverend Jones protects our company, those around us, and exorcises any human cursed to bear the unholy plague of possession."

Randall nodded, seemingly in agreement. "And the last man?"

"Hmmm. Master Lucian."

Hopkins knew for certain that across the town, the man known simply as Lucian would be found patrolling the darkness. He wore a similar pilgrim's hat to Hopkins, the same type of cape and dress code, waistcoat, cotton shirt, dark trousers and thick, heavy boots. Lucian wrapped his throat and face in a dark scarf, revealing only his eyes to the rest of the world. Long, black hair flowed beneath the brim of his hat. The cape wrapped tightly around, hiding the silver rapier buckled to his waist. Lucian's mastery of the weapon was legendary. Many a man, including those in service to the King's military, had fallen to this weapon and his mastery. A feat Hopkins had witnessed multiple times.

"Master Lucian is nothing more than a warrior in the Lord's name. His skill is exceptional. He has felled many lycanthropes, vampires and witches with his rapier, but also mortal men who simply annoy him, shall we say?"

"A master of swords who appears to be beyond control? How safe is my town?" Randall blurted.

"Settle, my good man," said Hopkins calmly, "he is no threat to you nor your people. He follows my every order and will do as I say."

"See to it that he does," Randall snapped, snatching his drink and finishing it in one. Hopkins simply smiled in return.

"We expect you and your men to begin at dawn," Mian added.

"Of course, and we will begin by investigating within the town itself. We must start with the people as there may still be disciples of the hag dwelling within the community. Should we be successful in destroying any disciples, the hag will ultimately lose her capacity to frighten your community, and will retire to the depths of the forest. This will be the quickest way to find the information we need and lead us to her, should we so need."

"And how will you do that?" Reverend Thomas enquired.

Hopkins smiled again. "My good man, leave that to me. If there is any information to be had about the witch amongst your people, we will extract it, of that you have my word."

A Fathers Love

Ellie's father took to logging in the early, crisp dawn. To the rest of the community he was known as Ted, the man who helped provide wood for fuel the year round. He worked in a patch of forest not far from the Elkwood boundary, and took with him a horse and wooden cart that creaked and moaned as it crossed the bumpy terrain. Ted had been joined by Sam, a fellow logger and friend. The two of them worked, undeterred by the stories of the hag haunting the forest. Their role within the community was extremely important, and whether they were afraid or not, they had to do their job. In truth, Ted was not afraid, simply cautious about the stories and his surroundings.

The loggers worked closely in the dull light. The foggy night had given way to a dawn untainted by mist. The sun crept from the horizon away to the east, its latent warmth unable to penetrate the cold, English winter. Stars remained above them, watching from afar as the two men worked laboriously within the dense pines. The echoes of their hatchets resonated between the trunks of those yet untouched around them as they chopped the fallen in to smaller pieces.

"How's your daughter?" Sam asked his workmate. After Ellie's nightmare and the strange quake felt in her home, news had spread fast amongst the townsfolk by those closest enough to witness it. Rumour began to circulate, and deep down Sam was concerned, especially as Mayor Randall was keeping the company of one Matthew Hopkins.

Ted stopped momentarily, keeping his gaze fixed upon the log he was about to chop. His breath puffed from his mouth and dispersed in the morning air.

"Fine," he replied, smashing his hatchet down, slicing a log clean in half. Sam continued to watch his friend working. Ted placed another log on the frozen ground and chopped it swiftly in one blow.

"Really?" he asked, his voice clearly concerned. Ted sighed again and clasped the tool in both hands. "The people talk," Sam began, feeling as though he should justify his enquiry.

Ted nodded slowly. "I know." His expression bore the look of a man concerned.

"I'm just worried for you. For you both. With everything happening around here, werewolves, lycanthropes, whatever you want to call them, ghosts, witchcraft and witchfinders, it doesn't take much for our townsfolk to let imagination and reality blur."

Ted offered nothing in reply. They stood silently. Even as the sun continued its upward trajectory, the cold air showed no sign of vanishing.

"I am worried for her safety, Sam, dreadfully worried," Ted said quietly. "Something is happening to her and I think it might be the same as, well..."

"Do you think it is possession or witchcraft?"

"I don't believe in witchcraft, Sam, not witchcraft as you know. Spells are a myth. Curses are legends. No one can create them simply by uttering a few words or twiddling a few fingers. Witchcraft is an excuse given to execute women who do not conform to the rules of the town. I believe our esteemed visitor Matthew Hopkins is using it as an easy way to earn himself wealth."

"Really?"

"Indeed." Who would dare question his authority when he works on behalf of Parliament? He has a free pass to commit whatever it is he desires and not one of us dare question or challenge him."

"So what do you intend doing?"

Ted paused. "I'm taking her away. Tonight."

Beginning

"Is this her? Is this the accused?" Hopkins shouted above the angry people flocked to the morning madness of the town. Their anger coiled about him like an enraged serpent as accusations of witchcraft swept through their community once more.

"That's her! That's her!"

"She's a witch!"

"Witch!"

Hopkins' accomplice, John Stearne, had hold of a young maiden by the hair.

Hopkins turned to Mayor Randall. "Master Randall?"

"This is her, Master Hopkins. This is the Miss Clark, who it is claimed is in league with the Devil."

"It's not me! It's not me! I am not a witch!" she screamed frantically, battling against Stearne's grip.

"It's never you, is it!" a female voice bellowed above the masses.

"It isn't me! I have nothing to do with the Devil or the Dark Arts! I haven't done anything wrong!"

Hopkins turned back to the accused. "But the entire town has pointed the finger at you, Miss. How may so many people be wrong? All of them are your accusers." The onlookers cheered.

"They are wrong! They're lying! I didn't do anything!"

"That's just your problem! You never do anything!" Part of the crowd roared again, this time in laughter as a male voice shouted exactly what he thought.

Hopkins smiled and studied the woman, who shedded tears. On her chin existed a mole. A thought then crossed his mind. "Master Lucian!" he bellowed across the baying mob. "Please bring to me the tool to Teat."

"I'm not a witch! It's not me! It's her! She's the witch! Her over there!"

The accused Miss Clark pointed towards woman standing at the front of the crowd. "She's the one, not me! It's her! I saw her do it! I saw her! You'll believe me now, won't you?"

"The liar!" the woman screamed in retaliation. "She's lying!"

The accused argued her innocence. "I've seen her! I've seen her summoning the Devil and scheming with the hag in the woods!"

Hopkins took the small, blunt needle that Lucian offered. "And grab her," he ordered. The crowd descended into a single, frenzied entity force. Many pushed the newly accused from her place amongst them. The terrified woman attempted to escape between the mass of bodies, but the townspeople blocked and pushed her back toward the Witchfinder. Lucian took hold of the woman's collar from behind and yanked her from the crowd, which in turn roared in cheer.

"Bring her here," the Witchfinder ordered through the profanities, and asked Mayor Randall the name of the newly accused.

"Hogarth. Miss Hogarth," Randall muttered. Hopkins knew from the tremble in his voice the Mayor was dismayed, possibly with more revelations from the community.

"A common trait in witches is the reluctance to take responsibility for their actions. Miss Clark, the way in which you will do anything to pass blame to others is unlike any I have ever witnessed before. It is sickening how you shirk your responsibility to other members of the community when you do something yourself that requires accountability. It is clear that this is how you have led your life thus far. The crowd even detests you, but I admit at being less than surprised, seeing how you have blamed everyone else for your own wrong doing. You will be trialed, regardless of your plea. And you, Miss Hogarth, you have been accused of witchcraft by one of your very own coven. How do you plead?"

"Guilty! Guilty!" cried the sea of people upon Hopkins played.

"I am not a witch! She is a witch and a liar!" Miss Hogarth cried.

"I am not, you liar!" Miss Clark retaliated. The crowd aired its anger.

"Kill them! Kill them!" came the odd scream through the thunder of voices.

Hopkins turned to Stearne and rolled his eyes. "Let's get this done, shall we?"

Stearne grinned. "You want a confession from this one?" he asked, swaying from side to side as Miss Clark struggled against him.

"No. Let's show these people how we reach our conclusions in the appropriate manner." Hopkins turned his attention to the masses. "My good people," he shouted. "Good citizens of Elkwood, may I have your blessed attention for a moment please?" The townspeople began to hush as the Witchfinder proceeded against the women. "We will know if Miss Clark is indeed a witch using this simple needle," he explained, raising the needle in the air. "Upon her chin there lays a teat. We will cut this teat with the needle. Should she bleed she will be innocent of all charges and accusations made against her. However, if she does not feel the needle, or if the teat fails to bleed, then she will be one in league with the Devil and will meet the punishment of death!"

The crowd roared. Hopkins knew the town wanted both women slaughtered, innocent or not. He turned back to the struggling Miss Clark and grasped her jaw with his hand. "Now, let us see," he whispered, jamming the needle in to her mole. The woman screamed as the object broke her skin. Hopkins withdrew it immediately and looked at the puncture. He looked at Stearne. "Bind her hands," the Witchfinder ordered. Stearne laughed and kicked the woman to her knees.

"Bring me rope!" Stearne bellowed out in to the crowd. "We have a witch!"

Miss Clark began to wail and struggled more vigorously. She lurched and fell against Stearne, knocking him into the wooden doors of a barn. The crowd, entertained by her actions, began to laugh. Hopkins raged.

"Devil!" Stearne snapped angrily, smacking the back of her head. Miss Clark's head rolled to the side. Her sobbing subsided.

"No, Master Stearne. Not quite."

Hopkins dived to the floor as Stearne flew into the crowd. Screams and cries lifted from those who broke his fall before buckling beneath his weight. Miss Clark turned to Hopkins, her eye sockets pale, her skin colourless and taught. The pupils in both eyes vanished leaving nothing more than whites. Her teeth protruded as she smiled toward him.

"Demon!" Hopkins screamed across the chaos. The demon bellowed with a deep, guttural laugh and lifted a hand to attack the Witchfinder. A whistle sounded through the air. The creature's hand jerked backward as an arrow ploughed through its palm, stapling it to the barn door behind. The demon screamed, writhing in an attempt to free itself. Daniel Wade pushed through to join his company. "Father!" Hopkins bellowed, looking for his company's clergyman. Wade took aim again and fired again, slicing the demon's free arm. The creature groaned, now pinned against the wooden door with no means of escape.

Hopkins found Reverend Jones emerge through the chaotic crowds, hurriedly flickering through the pages of his bible. "The Lord is my shepherd, wherefore I lack nothing. He maketh me lie down in green pastures…" The demon squirmed as it looked upward into the sky.

"Hurry up!" Hopkins shouted above the ensuing chaos. Through the stampeding bodies and terrified townspeople he saw Miss Hogarth making her getaway. Hopkins snapped his fingers and alerted Lucian, pointing in her direction.

"He leadeth me beside quiet waters, He refreshes my soul…" Jones continued as he emerged from the melee.

The demon snarled angrily and spat towards the clergyman.

Hopkins watched as Lucian drew a knife from beneath his cape and grasped it by the blade. The hunter tracked the fleeing accused with both his left arm and finger outstretched. With a swift movement he released the weapon from his fingers. Miss Hogarth screamed as the knife embedded itself in her lower back, sending her tumbling to the ground. Stearne powered through the flooding bodies and fought his way across.

"He guideth me along the paths of righteousness for His name's sake…"

The demon screamed and shook its head from side-to-side, attempting in vain to escape the arrows that pierced its body. "You bastard! You bastard!" It began, spewing dark liquid from its mouth as it screamed the profanity.

Hopkins laid eyes upon Mayor Randall. He leapt across to the dignitary. "Master Randall! Master Randall! Summon your executioner immediately! *Immediately!*"

"Yes! Yes!" Randall muttered. He turned to the townspeople. "Summon the executioner!"

"Yea though I walk through the darkest valley…" Jones' voice wavered above the general mayhem. Hopkins returned his attention to the creature. "I fear no evil, for thou art with me…"

The demon shrieked, terrifying the townspeople. "Death will come for you, Master William Jones! He's coming for you!" The creature wailed from its crucifixion. Jones stopped praying , peering momentarily over the abomination affixed to the hefty wooden door. Hopkins watched as a mixture of dark liquid and blood frothed from the demon's mouth. "Yes, Reverend Jones. Death will come for you when you least expect it, of that I will make certain."

"Pay no attention, Reverend. The demon attempts to cloud your mind," Hopkins ordered. He kept his cool within the chaos.

Jones nodded once. His expression of nervousness did not fill Hopkins with great confidence. "Thy rod and Thy staff, they comfort me." The demon hocked and spat upon the clergyman, then laughed defiantly. Slowly the creature began dragging its pierced palm through the silver shafted arrow. Blood cascaded from the injury

down upon the arm and on to the cotton dress it was wearing.
Through the air flew another arrow, this time embedding the demon
beneath the wrist it was moving. Hopkins turned to see his marksman,
Daniel Wade, approach closer. The demon cried.

"Thou preparest a table for me in the presence of my enemies..."
Wind ruffled the page from which Jones was reading. "Thou anointest
my head with oil; my cup overfloweth ..."

Hopkins heard the sound of scraping across the cobbled ground.
Through the hysteria the hulking figure of the executioner emerged,
dragging the heavy, silver-tipped axe behind. "Let him through!" The
Witchfinder ordered. "Let him pass!" The townspeople parted to
allow the hooded figure free access to the Witchfinder.

Jones prayed onward. "Surely thy goodness and love will follow
me all the days of my life..."

"When he finishes, hack the creature in to pieces. Understand?"
Hopkins ordered the executioner. The blackened hood nodded just
once.

"And I will dwell in the house of the Lord forever. Amen."
Reverend Jones made the sign of the cross with his free hand.
The demon screamed.

Hopkins pointed. "Now!"

The axe hung high in the air long enough for the demon to focus
on the blunted edge. With one sweep the blade fell, smashing the
wooden door and severing the creature in half from head to toe. Blood
and organs leaked onto the ground and spilled out towards the masses.
The executioner swung again, severing the already decapitated body
in to smaller pieces.

Hopkins showed no emotion as the axe bludgeoned the body to
nothing more than red mush and pulp. Blood squirted into the air.
Some landed on Hopkins face. The Witchfinder watched the
execution intently whilst wiping it from his cheek.

The town fell silent. The executioner had completed his task. The wind swept about the hunters, bellowing their capes in various directions.

John Stearne and Lucian thrust the injured Miss Hogarth to the ground at Hopkins' feet. He looked down on the woman from beneath the rim of his hat.

"What should we do with this one?" Stearne asked.

Hopkins mused a moment or so, looking over the sobbing woman. He turned his attention to the executioner, and subtly gestured his head sideways in her direction. The executioner nodded, lifting his axe in the air once more. Hopkins and his men stepped away from the accused to allow room for the executioner to ply his trade. With another swift movement the axe fell, plunging down upon the hapless woman.

Master Mian

The cold winter's day sparkled with clear sunshine but as yet it held no warmth. As the day progressed it rose higher in the cloudless skies then dwindled in the early evening twilight. Hopkins and his men canvassed the town followed unenthusiastically by the town's officials. Hopkins was as callous as the reputation that preceded him and was more brutal than anyone could have ever imagined. As the day continued the remainder of the women trialled for witchcraft were found not guilty, and with a demon and witch both executed, the threat of the illusive hag haunting the woods dwindled to nothing more than folklore. Hopkins explained to everyone that the hag would no longer hold any influence now that her minions had perished, and the community cheered. There was, however, talk of one who remained un-trialled, and the Witchfinder listened with great interest at the stories the peasants were relaying to him.

Master Mian had heard stories of Hopkins on his rare jaunts to London before the curse befell Elkwood, although never admitted to anyone he knew of the hunter's reputation. After all, tales of his murderous conquest and escapades made for compelling listening, and it was during these trips that Mian had discovered that some people, even Parliament members for that matter, believed Hopkins had killed men and women in the name of witchcraft simply to make money, regardless of their innocence or guilt. It was an easy way, Mian thought as he wandered behind this strange group of hunters, to make vast sums of money with little evidence. After all, in a small town such as Elkwood, who would know for sure the signs and symptoms of witchcraft except through accusation? Of course, a person who used their left hand predominantly was certain to be accused of being a witch, as was anyone using herbs or vegetation to cure ailments, but what other signs could there be? Yes, it was easy for a so-called expert to visit the town and charge anything he wanted to rid its occupants of the cursed problem. People would believe whatever the Witchfinder told them when they were ridden with anxiety, and with the recent werewolf attack and witch burning, fear was indeed great within this community. It was a town in need of a saviour, and at this particular moment Hopkins was indeed that saviour. The people were afraid. Anyone could be accused and trialled and there would be no-one there to fight their cause. Hopkins was still on the hunt for a witch, and as the day dragged onward, it was only a matter of time before he found another. At least, that was the thought of Master Mian, the cold and angry gentleman following at the end of the group.

Uninvited

Ted arrived at home as the sun began to set. The wood he'd been working hard to provide lay inside the wagon next to the house. The horse was settled in the small stable behind, and after a long day of logging he was finally ready to sit beside a warm fire and rest his weary body.

After a meal of poultry and bread he sat in a chair created by his own hand and finally began to relax, thinking about the plan. He would take Ellie and leave at dawn. If he left during the hours of daybreak with the horse and wagon the sentries on duty would be more likely to believe he was heading out to begin his work. Tired, he began to doze. The fire popped, sending an ember into the air and bringing him back to consciousness. Ellie was sitting beside its warmth at his feet. Now fully awake, he sat up in the chair, gaining her attention.

"What's wrong?" Ellie asked quietly.

"Wrong?" he asked, yawning as he did so, "what makes you believe anything is wrong?"

Ellie took a poker in her hand and prodded the firewood. "I can tell," she replied, not turning to address her father.

"Nothing's wrong."

"Don't lie, father, I know."

Ted sighed. What was wrong? How about the fact she was too much like her mother? That was what was wrong.

They sat in silence. Ted wondered whether to tell Ellie what was planned, or spring it on her when he intended to go. The fire cracked as the flames grew, and he watched Ellie's face dance with various shades of amber in its light.

"It was another dream yesterday," she began, again keeping her eyes away from her fathers, "about mother. The same thing. Fire.

50

Death. I'm sure that a lady of twenty one and a half years should not be dreaming things of this nature. Do you?"

Ted sighed. His thoughts were the same. "No Ellie, I do not," he answered softly.

"When I dream, terrible things happen. Glass and pottery smash. Doors burst open. And yesterday, the house shook. It *shook*. But not only the house, the grounds surrounding us. People saw. You saw," she said, finally looking up to him. Ted found her eyes holding back tears, but more troubling, they clearly showed apprehension, even terror.

"Father, what is happening to me?"

"Ellie," he said, smiling gently and placing a hand on her shoulder, "you're too much like your mother."

"My mother?"

"Yes. Your mother was an amazing person, so full of life, and love for that matter. She went through the same thing whilst bearing you. Whatever it is, it connects you both, and you should be grateful for it."

"Then maybe I must find her," Ellie wiped a tear from her cheek. "You said she left when I was a baby, maybe I should look for her?"

Ted removed his hand and sat back in the chair. He knew this time would come, eventually. After twenty one and a half of years, the protective silence he kept might now be appropriately broken. The truth about her mother may help his daughter to understand what she was experiencing.

"Ellie, there is something I must tell you," he began slowly. "Your mother? She... she didn't leave."

"What?"

"She didn't leave us. She..."

Three thuds on the wooden of their home brought and abrupt end to the conversation. "I don't believe it," Ted seethed, rising from his seat. "If this is that McDonald lad for you I'll shove that pitchfork up his-"

"Good evening. Mr Harewood." Ted's heart skipped. Matthew Hopkins stood ominously before him, grinning manically from beneath his hat. "In fact, it is not yourself with whom I seek to converse, but rather your beautiful daughter."

"What?" Ted mustered, emotion overcoming reason. Behind Hopkins he could see many townsfolk, some carrying torches in the freezing air, as well as the town dignitaries. Mayor Randall pushed past Hopkins and gently took hold of him on both arms.

"Ted, it's for the best."

Realisation set in. "No! NO!"

Lucian smashed Ted's throat with a forearm, pinning him against the door. Ted struggled and fought back.

"Settle down old man, or my blade will feast on your flesh." Lucian hid behind the scarf. His blue eyes pierced Ted's with meaning and intent.

"I'm sorry," Randall whispered. Ted struggled again but this time could not muster the strength against Lucian's power.

"Kill her!" came a voice from outside. "Kill the witch!" Cheering began amongst the followers. Ted watched helplessly as John Stearne entered the house to find his daughter. Stearne smiled, wiping his hands across an already soiled tunic. "Hello my love." Ellie jumped to her feet. Stearne tackled the girl to the floor, knocking her head against exposed boards which laid her cold.

"NO!" Ted's word garbled as Lucian held him by the throat, forcing his jaw upwards. "One more peep from you, Master Harewood, and you'll be joining her."

Stearne laughed as he slung Ellie's unconscious body over his shoulder and stomped past Ted to the crowd outside. "GOT HER!" he shouted ecstatically. The crowd erupted with a cheer and began chanting.

"She made the ground shake!" Ted heard one voice scream.

"The houses shook!" came another.

"Kill her!"

"Ted, you must remain calm, or they'll kill you too," Randall advised.

"Wise words from your friend," Lucian agreed. "I suggest you listen to him." Lucian released Ted from the hold and left after Stearne, his cape flowing as he vanished. "We've known for a long time, Ted, a very long time," Randall explained, speaking courteously to the logger. "I've been able to keep it quiet until now, out of respect for you, but when the ground rumbles and the buildings quake, I can't ignore it. You can't ignore it. She is too dangerous-"

"Then let her leave!" Ted shouted, attempting to push past.

"No, no, no, remember your warning. Don't let us lose the both of you for this crime, please. You knew this day would come sooner or later."

"She's no harm, to you or to anyone!" Ted pushed past the Mayor and out in to the winter night. The executioner stood amongst the crowd, his dark hood an object of terror for those who witnessed it. But even he was a mere onlooker: it was the professionals who held control over the situation. Ellie's body waved with the movement of Stearne's pace as he made his way toward the square with her over his shoulder. The square meant one thing. Fire. Ted's vision flashed. His nose excruciated blunt pain.

"Restrain him," Hopkins ordered. Lucian punched him back into line, and was now grasped on both arms by Daniel Wade and Reverend Jones.

Ted looked at the clergyman. "Will a man of the cloth see the needless death of a young woman?" Blood ran from his broken nose through his moustache and onto his lips.

"It's not a needless death, my friend, but a welcome one. She will return to the darkness whence she came."

"Shut up!" Daniel ordered Ted, "or you'll be killed too! Keep quiet, for God's sake!"

"ELLIE!" came another scream. Ted looked to see Jack McDonald forcing his way through the crowds. He launched at

Stearne, his hands poised ready to fight, but was felled and restrained by the hooded executioner.

"Randall!" Ted shouted, slowly gaining his senses. "Randall!" Ted's restrainers motioned him to move forward.

"Ted, I'm sorry," came Randall's response through the crowds.

"Randall, no. Not like this. I beg you. Please? For everything I have done for this town. Not by fire. Not again."

The crowd worked themselves into frenzy. Ted saw them slapping and punching the head of his daughter. "NO!" he screamed angrily.

"Shut up!" Wade whispered again. "If you value your life you'll keep your mouth closed!"

"WAIT!" Randall shouted at the top of his voice, halting the procession. "WAIT!"

The angry mob turned to their Mayor, their voices diminishing to silence. Stearne turned to face him, as did Hopkins. "What is it, my good man?" the Witchfinder asked.

"Do what you must," Randall began hesitantly, "but not like this. Not in this most painful and barbaric of ways."

Hopkins laughed softly. "This young lady has been found guilty of witchcraft by your own people, and you do not wish her dead?"

"I do, but not in such a barbaric manner."

"And why, may I ask, is that?"

"Because both Ellie and her father have served this township well during their years here. They're not like the hag, nor the woman we burned two nights past. These two people have helped our town to exist and flourish. *She* helped our town. If she is to die, she should do so in as painless and as quick a way as possible."

"Please," Ellie sobbed, "I don't want to die."

"Shut up!" Stearne ordered.

Jack went for Stearne and was once more restrained by the hooded giant. "Bastard! I'll kill you!"

Hopkins looked between both Ted and Jack, fighting for the honour of the so-called witch. "Well, it seems we have some sort of a predicament." Ted peered at the bodies surrounding him and his captors. "It is certain that the witch must die, but it would appear she has two people cast under her spell. Let her down a moment," Hopkins ordered. Stearne complied and dropped Ellie to the ground, causing her to cough upon impact. He grabbed the linen dress she wore and yanked her up, restrained her with both arms around the waist, and pulled her on tip toe. "Mayor Randall, I agree whole heartedly with what you say. People who have served the town well should indeed be considered when anything of this nature arises. However, it would appear that three people will now be executed on two counts. One, suspicion of witchcraft, and two, the harbouring of a witch."

Ted growled. "Mayor Randall," began Hopkins, "I hear your request, and I will also spare the lives of the two men in question, on one condition."

"And what may that be?" Randall asked.

"She will not be burned, and these men will not die, if…"

"If what?" Jack shouted.

"If," Hopkins repeated, turning to Jack and then again to Randall, "both of the men disassociate themselves from the witch."

The crowd erupted. Ellie cried. Ted struggled. Ted watched as Hopkins made his way across toward Ellie's young lover. With a leather glove he grabbed Jack's chin and raised it upwards. "Now, heed me, lad. I will ask you questions and you will answer. Your answers will not only determine your own fate, but that of the girl as well. Now I will ask you; do you, or have you ever, participated in witchcraft or the dark arts in your short life?"

Ted began to pray. "No," Jack gasped.

"Hmm. And if you renounce the dark arts, what then must you accuse Ellie Harewood of being?"

"No," Jack whispered.

"No is not an answer, squire, now tell me what she is!"

"No!"

"Jack?" Ted listened as Ellie's voice drift across the air.

"Your life is on the line! Her execution is now upon your conscience!" Hopkins shouted, pointing towards Ellie, "and a painful death awaits her if you do not say it! Now tell me!"

Jack snatched his chin from Hopkins' grasp and dropped his head. He began to sob. Raising his head upright, tears streaming down his face, he said it. Ted's heart sank.

"Witch," he whispered. "Ellie is a witch."

"Jack?" Ellie sobbed.

"Excellent!" Hopkins clasped his hands together. "This brave young man goes free!"

Jack found hands patting his shoulders and ruffling his hair. "Well done, lad. Well done," was the praise emerging from the community.

"No," Ellie sighed.

"Now, Master Harewood." Hopkins wandered slowly back between the torches and lanterns to Ted. "I will ask you the same question. Do you, or have you ever, participated in witchcraft or the dark arts in your life?"

"Father!" Ellie shouted across to him.

Ted looked at her and then to Hopkins. "Go to Hell," he replied defiantly.

Hopkins smiled. "Not before your daughter, Master Harewood, of that you have my word. And how she gets there is of your own choosing."

"Bastard!"

"Last chance before she is burned alive and you are forced to watch." The smile had vanished from Hopkins' face and replaced with an expression Ted found terrible to behold. "Her eyes will meet yours as she burns, as she cries out to you, asking you why, why did you do this? You will see her roast, see her flesh darken and crumble, see her die in the most painful of ways. Her last moments on earth will be the worst of her life, and it will be of your own doing. And then, Master Harewood, you will join her. I will leave the choice of your execution to the fearsome fellow clad in the black hood. I believe he is partial to dismemberment using his great axe. Now, do I need to ask my friend Mr Stearne to stoke up the firewood?"

Ted's eyes welled with tears. "No," he said gently, "no. I have never taken part in witchcraft at all during my life."

Hopkins' smile returned. "And if you totally renounce the dark arts, what then must you accuse your daughter, Ellie Harewood, of being?"

"Father? FATHER!"

"A witch," he said quietly. "A witch."

"At last!" Hopkins shouted over the cheers of the crowd, "we have our confessions! Ellie Harewood has been denounced by those closest to her!"

"Kill her!"

"Kill her!" came the voice of the townsfolk through the bitter air.

"NO. NO!" Ellie screamed.

Hopkins slapped Ted's shoulder. "Well done, it takes courage to turn over a witch, especially when she is of your own flesh and blood. You will go free, and no one in this town will judge you any longer. As a result of your honesty your daughter will be executed by a method known as 'weathering.' She will be taken to the depths of the forest and bound to a tree . The cold will eventually freeze her to death, but not before it sends her to a deep slumber. You have my word it is the least painful of ways to be executed."

"Well done," Mayor Randall added, "you did what is best."

"Indeed you did," Hopkins confirmed, "for you, for the boy, and of course for your daughter. Stearne!" he shouted, turning to face his cohort. "Weathering!"

"Weathering it is!" Stearne acknowledged.

Ted took one last look at his daughter before being dragged to her fate. Ellie stared back at him without flinching. What he saw in her face was anger. Anger, and evil.

Weathering

The townsfolk accompanied Hopkins and his men as they went into the forest. Stearne carried Ellie over his shoulder, as he had when marching to the square. Ellie's hands and feet were bound with rope. The townspeople carried flames which illuminated the night, many screaming obscenities in her direction, following Stearne in much the same way as mice followed the pied piper. She cried, looking back at the mass of people detesting her. Matthew Hopkins was first in her eye line followed by Mayor Randall and Father Thomas. The rest of Hopkins' group followed, creating a barrier between the dignitaries and commoners. The air filled with anger and false bravado. Commoners feared anything they could not explain, and welcomed any murder or trial that would ward off superstitions.

Onward they continued, the forest floor becoming more treacherous as they ventured in to the wilderness. Stearne stumbled, rolling Ellie momentarily, but continued his journey, oblivious to the surroundings. "Up there," a man's voice echoed. Ellie watched as Hopkins took a torch from the crowd and entered the open space. His flame's light revealed a mighty oak tree, isolated in a clearing. The tree had died an age ago, and its branches, shrivelled and sharp, protruded from the backdrop of the forest.

"Master Stearne," Hopkins shouted, "this will suffice."

Stearne followed Hopkins' orders and entered the clearing with Lucian. Ellie gave up the fight, too exhausted to continue. The remaining members of the Witchfinder's company restrained the townspeople, allowing Ellie to be subjected to that of which she had been found guilty. She slumped to the ground and cried out as Stearne released the hold.

"Shut up!" he growled, slapping her head. The slap echoed through the emptiness and brought the townspeople to a silence.

"Bastard!" Ted shouted. Ellie sensed her father attempt to break free from the mob.

"Settle, Master, or he will execute the both of you," Wade's voice emerged. "There's not much point in both of you being killed."

Ellie squealed as Stearne took a handful of hair, forcing her upright and against the tree. Lucian drew thick rope around her midriff which restricted Ellie's breathing to short, sharp gasps. They wrapped the rope around the trunk several times before finally tying the knot and securing the witch in place. Stearne grabbed Ellie and attempted to slack the binding. The rope refused to budge.

"We're done here," he said, looking over to Hopkins. Hopkins did nothing more than nod, his face obscured from Ellie's vision by the rim of his hat. Reverend Thomas offered one last prayer to the woman. "Goodbye, poppet," Stearne laughed as he left the clearing. Ellie sobbed. As the men disappeared she noticed Ted watching from beside the Mayor, and her sadness turned to anger. She narrowed her eyes and snarled to him.

"I hate you!" she screamed across the clearing. "I hate you!"

"Carry on," Hopkins stated, "there is nothing more to see here now."

"I hate you!"

Her anger intensified as she watched Randall place a hand on his back, as though her father was a hero to the people.

***

The last thing Ted heard was the terrified sobs of his daughter, drifting through the darkness and the bitter winter's night.

Ellie watched as the flares disappear between the trees. Now she was alone in the open and had been left to die. She cried through fear of the surroundings and of her own mortality, until the forest resonated with silence and the isolation became apparent. Anger replaced fear and she began to shout and in to the darkness, cursing for what seemed an eternity before succumbing to exhaustion. Afraid once more, the warmth generated by her exertions decreased and gave way to the cold. The temperature fell further, as shivers passed up and down her back. Goosebumps tingled with each gust of wind. Then, almost simultaneously, a powerful, sharp sensation emerged inside her fingers and toes. The sky above was as clear as a crystal with stars flickering clearly as she gasped in the cold air. A tiny spot of frost cracked upon her neck as she moved.

Ellie's breathing grew faster. The stinging in her toes more uncomfortable. Moving the digits was near impossible. Her fingers did not tingle as much as the toes, and she noted her thighs becoming numb. A shiver passed between the shoulders. She moved as much as the ropes allowed. Ellie tingled with every small movement whilst attempting to keep her body warm. The cold air stung with each breath. Every movement stabbed. Her vision distorted with frost that now settled on her lashes. The cotton dress cracked with each movement as it froze. The tingling sensation turned to burning, and no matter what, the pain would not go. Ellie became light headed and felt her heartbeat weaken. The breeze stabbed relentlessly at her freezing body. She looked up to the sky as a tear emerge from the corner of her eye. It trickled to her cheek and stopped, frozen in its track.

Ellie jolted from slumber. Shivering, she strained to see out in to the darkness. The overwhelming, tingling sensation burned constantly. Her dress crackled throughout the clearing. Frost broke as she moved, settling where exposed skin had once been. Ice sealed where mucus had formed, forcing a breath to be gasped from the mouth. Her right eyelid strained to open, bonded together by the elements. Pain in her fingers had spread to the wrists and ankles. A sharp sensation sliced from inside her body. Ellie opened her mouth but passed out, her body finally falling to the winter's night.

She jolted to consciousness. Her body screamed and burned. Ellie surrendered to the biting winds and freezing air which was taking her life. She could not move, not even to twitch a finger. She was freezing, and knew it. To pass out once more would almost certainly bring with it the eternal slumber. Unable to withstand the elements any further, Ellie accepted her fate, closed her eyes and fell unconscious.

Death

Dawn broke across the forest. Frozen through, and hanging away from the tree to which she had been bound, the body of Ellie Harewood hung lifeless. Crows infested the branches above the body, cawing and squealing in the early morning sun as they awaited the one whom was destined to transport her to the other side.

"Well, well, what have we here?" came a scratchy old voice from across the clearing. There emerged a small, hunched, shuffling figure, cloaked from head to foot. The footfalls the figure made crunched across the frozen vegetation as it moved slowly towards the tree and girl tied to it. The cloaked figure raised its small arms and flapped them toward the branches. "Shoo, go on now, get out!" it shouted, distressing the crows. The murder squealed and cawed but did as the figure ordered, scattering from the oak and settling themselves within the trees close to the opening. The cloak stopped in front of the oak tree and an old, wrinkled hand emerged from its depth. A long finger reached out and prodded the head of the girl. Gaining no response, the dirty hand reached out and took hold of the frozen hair, lifting upwards to reveal the girl's features. "You're not dead, not yet." The hood looked toward the crows perched around the clearing. "They would all but be gone now if you had passed."

Hidden eyes studied the body. The figure felt something strange, almost surreal. It felt as though it knew the woman bound here in the frozen forest. It knew they had never met, but still, a connection was there. A strange sensation of power passed inside the figure's hand, power that emanated from this woman dying in the cold. The feeling increased, surging now into the body. This sensation was something that the cloak recognised, and stepped back in disbelief. "Such power…"

The girl roused to consciousness and lifted her head with an apparent effort. "H-h-h-h-h-h-h-h-"

"Shush, child, do not speak. Do not be afraid, I will help you."

"Sorry, it's a little late for that," a voice emerged from across the opening. The figure turned to see a man dressed in garments it had never before seen. He was only young, maybe of thirty years or a little more, and wore black trousers and shoes, a tattered, red waistcoat, and a red sash that hung from his waist. The cloak could see he was protected from the cold by a long, black overcoat that divided into tails. On his head rested a tall top hat set slightly to one side.

"You?" the cloak asked, "what are you doing here?"

"Ah, Sister Luna, what a pleasant surprise," the man began as he crossed the frozen ground. "How is it that whenever I'm called to this particular year and this particular part of the world, I usually encounter you?"

Sister Luna removed her hood, allowing her long, dirty grey hair to be revealed. "What clothing is that which you bear?"

"Ah, this?" he asked, opening his coat. "This comes from the year eighteen ninety eight. I took it from a shop owner I was accompanying across the plains. Very dapper, isn't it?" He twirled with an open jacket. "Unfortunately I doubt you'll live over two hundred and forty years to see the likes of this for yourself."

"Indeed I will not. I wonder what sights you have seen on your journeys?"

"Let me tell you, I've seen some amazing things. This job is great, you know, travelling across time and seeing every type of civilisation known to man."

"But you're nothing more than a tradesman," Sister Luna said bluntly.

The man tipped his hat. "Indeed I am, but a good one at that."

"Then I take it you've come here for her?" Luna nodded towards the body on the tree.

"Indeed I have, Sister Luna, indeed I have. A young soul like hers should be worth a bob or two to both buyers."

"And you do this without regard for her eternal peace?"

"Unfortunately, it's just the way the world is these days. Nine times out of ten I'll take them to the right crossing, because that's my job, but sometimes you get some people who are just so evil, so nasty and unpleasant I take them straight downstairs. On the occasions when both lords want a soul I carry, I open a bidding war. Whoever gives me what I want, wins. Simple as that. I'm taking an educated guess that she'll be of interest to both parties, what with her powers and all."

"Yes, I did notice," Luna replied, turning her attention to the unconscious woman. "She's not dead, yet. Not until you touch her. Release her to my care. She still has much to offer this world."

The man laughed. "Oh, Sister Luna, I do love meeting with you, you make my day sometimes, you know that?"

"Release her to me, Samael; she's too young and valuable."

"Sister," said Samael, placing his hands on his waist, "she is worth more to me than anything else I can lay my hands upon. I'm not going to give her up, I'm sorry. Now, if you'll excuse me, I've got a soul to take."

He waltzed past.

"Wait! You like to bargain, don't you?"

"Usually, yes, but not today I'm afraid. I'm due elsewhere very soon."

"Wait! How about this? You said she's valuable to you? What if we increase the souls you take? More souls mean more bargaining for the two worlds to joust over."

Samael sighed and turned. He folded his arms. "Alright, you have my attention, but only briefly." The tails to his jacket flapped in a brief gust of wind.

"Release her to me, to do as I please, and in return I'll make sure she delivers more souls to you in exchange for her own."

Samael frowned. "How many?" he asked. Luna knew instantly that he was intrigued by the thought.

"How much is she worth to you?"

Samael looked over his shoulder at the dying woman before meeting her gaze again. He tipped his head and raised his brows. "Could be in the region of twenty plus with the power she has. Can you imagine what him downstairs would do with that? And because of the threat she would pose, him upstairs would probably want to get her safely to his world so she doesn't become an enemy. Could even be more, but I'd say firmly she's worth twenty souls at least."

Sister Luna pondered the thought for a moment. "All right, I offer the following. Fifty souls in exchange for hers. Deal?"

"Fifty? Fifty souls?"

"She will kill fifty people; each one will take her place. How does that appeal?"

Samael gritted his teeth for a moment, clearly considering the offer. He looked about the trees and then up in to the clear sky. "Fifty souls. Very well, but they must all be delivered by her own hand, and no-one else. Should she deliver fewer souls they are still given to me as part of the debt. You have one month. Should she fail, I take the both of you as payment in full. Do we agree?"

Luna nodded. "We agree."

"Then she is yours to do with as you please." Samael clicked his fingers, and from the tree the young woman fell to the floor. The rope remained bound to the tree trunk. Samael approached Sister Luna. "You had best be sure she's trained and able to use her power. She won't be able to deliver on your promise otherwise. I'll be in contact with you both regularly to keep score on how many she delivers. You have until the last stage of the moon during the month of March to deliver the fifty. That will be when I appear to take the both of you across to the other side."

"There will be no need, of that I can promise."

"Then I will bid you good day, Sister, and look forward to our next meeting." Samael tipped his hat again and made his way across the opening. The crows launched into the air and followed their master as he disappeared along a trail into the forest.

Ellie looked up at the clear sky. A cloak appeared in her vision. Although rescued, she was exhausted. Unconsciousness took her once more, but not before a different, larger silhouette swooped down to grab her.

Order

"And so you see, Master Mian, your village is now protected from any supernatural threat that these women might have over your town and its good people," Matthew Hopkins explained as he took a sip from his warm drink on the cold winter's morn.

"And what of the lycanthropes? Do they not possess a threat now that young Ellie Harewood is frozen to a tree? You have done nothing to stop their onslaught."

Hopkins smiled his usual, demonic smile and placed his drink down. "Master Mian, I have simply done what your Mayor has requested." He pointed a hand across to Randall. "I was to find and execute your witch, which I have done successfully. I am a kind and generous man, and I know that your community cannot afford the price of lycanthrope slaughter on top of this."

"That is simply not the point," Mian said, his frustration with the Witchfinder abundantly clear. "We spoke at length about what exactly our town would be paying you for, and you extolled the expertise of one of your company in hunting lycanthropes. I simply will not allow you to leave without ridding our lands of all the accursed!"

"Master Mian!" Hopkins shouted, his patience with these simple townsfolk finally exhausted, "there are no longer any witches within your community! Now that the Harewood girl is destroyed the hag will hold little power over the town! The demon that plagued your people has been exorcised and destroyed before your very eyes! Did you not see the putrid filth pouring from its mouth as the good Reverend recited a passage from the Bible? Did you not see her unholy body diced by your very own executioner? During my cull we trialled and executed two witches and a demon, and you worry about lycanthropes? The demon has gone, and with it the attraction of anything unholy in your town! If the hag has not moved on from this you will remain as safe as you sit now! She will have no powers as such keeping curses hanging over you, as no more are likely to succumb to her influence. May I remind you that I work on behalf of His Majesty's Parliament. I have been appointed to rid the lands of witches who threaten the very well-being of our country's fine people! I will not be spoken to in such a manner! To insult me as you have is as good as insulting the good King himself! My company and I are leaving this very morning, with full payment for our services, whether you agree to it or not!"

Mian looked towards Mayor Randall. Randall moved his arm from the fireplace against which he was leaning. "Pay him," he ordered. "We can deal with the wolves ourselves. Send word to the blacksmith to forge weapons of silver tips before the moon is next full. Summon both Master York and Duggan from their labours. They are the best hunters within our town. They can hunt any rogues wandering near to our borders. But, Master Hopkins, will you guarantee that we will be left in peace from the witches whom torment us?"

"Of course. She will be weakened now that the two have been executed and the demon destroyed. The hag is unlikely to set eyes upon your town ever again. If she does, you are now in the position of power in which you can trial her yourselves in the same way as you have done the others so successfully." Hopkins didn't care much anymore for his perceived duty. He didn't care that the hag still roamed the forest. He cared only to move on to the next settlement to gain more payment. Promises were meant to be broken, and lies had always ensured his services rewarded. Randall shook his head before storming from the room. The treasurer turned to the Witchfinder. "How much?" Hopkins revelled in the success of his extortion.

"Thirty shillings, if you please."

"Thirty!" he shouted angrily, but Hopkins knew the treasurer was defeated.

Hopkins and his company trotted through the town and its people with Stearne at his side. His comrade leant across from the saddle to speak privately with his leader. Hopkins leant closer. "Be glad to get out of this pig sty. These people don't know what exactly it is we've done for them."

"Indeed, Master Stearne, you are correct. These simple peasants were hardly worth our time, although we did leave with more than is deemed usual."

"And how much did you charge them?"

The hooves of their horses thudded over the frozen grounds. "Considering their lack of intelligence I decided that our duty here should be rewarded handsomely. I charged them twenty."

Ten of those shillings charged to Mian found their way in to Hopkins' personal funds, the one he kept hidden from his company.

Stearne smiled. "You sly old apple-john!" Hopkins returned the smile.

"HALT!" a boomed from behind his company.

Hopkins closed his eyes in frustration. "What now?"

"Master Hopkins, sir," said Daniel from the rear.

"Halt in the name of the King!" Hopkins turned his steed to face a company of soldiers bearing the banners of their King, Charles the First. Mayor Randall and Reverend Thomas emerged into the square, likely to see what was happening. Mian had followed not long behind, clutching at the coppers, all that remained of the small town's treasury.

From the front of the company a soldier, clad in thick armour, dropped down from his horse. "Master Matthew Hopkins, I presume?"

"Indeed, your presumption is correct, sir. May I ask as to your business?" he enquired as he dismounted from his horse.

"Master Hopkins, Witchfinder General, I have been sent by His Majesty's Parliament to find you and issue this request, on behalf of His Majesty, King Charles the First."

"A request from the King? With regards to what?"

"Master Hopkins, may I ask who appointed your good self to work on behalf of our King's Parliament?"

Hopkins felt a flutter of nervousness. "Who would you think would employ me to such power?" he asked calmly, hiding his nerves from his company and the soldier.

"Master Hopkins, it has come to the attention of our good King that you are trialling and murdering these so-called witches in the name of Parliament, am I correct?"

Hopkins felt the attention of the townspeople and their dignitaries watching him. If he faltered now these simpletons would surely attack him for murdering the young woman and also for the amount he charged them for the service. "Indeed you are."

The soldier continued. "In light of your good work carried out in Parliament's name, the King has personally expressed a request to you, Master Hopkins."

"But of course. Anything for our gracious King." The Witchfinder bowed his head slightly.

"King Charles the First has requested that you bring with you the latest woman trialled by your hand for witchcraft. He wishes to have her examined by the royal physicians in London. Our King is intrigued by the work you are doing in his good name."

"As much as I would like to help, my most recent subject has now passed on," Hopkins explained, knowing that no-one could survive a harsh and cold night such as the Harewood girl had endured.

"That is acceptable. The King would then like you to return her body to London for examination."

"What?" Hopkins snapped. He turned to his company briefly, noticing them whispering to one another, except for Lucian. His warrior sat silently, hidden by a hat and scarf.

"That is the expressed wishes of the King. Who is in charge here?" the soldier asked as he looked around the square.

"I am, sir," Randall answered.

71

"And you are?"

"William James Randall. I am the Mayor of this good town."

"Mayor," the soldier greeted. He strolled across to the dignitary and placed some scrolls in his hand. "You are to write weekly to the King to let him know of Master Hopkins' progress. He is to deliver the body of the woman whom he speaks, to London, in no later than a month's time. Your correspondence will serve as vital information in his quest. The King expects a letter weekly and without fail. If you fail to write, we will be dispatched here to your fine township of Elkwood to discover exactly why you have not written, and if the answer is deemed unsatisfactory you will answer in your defence to parliament and King Charles himself." The soldier then turned back to Hopkins. "Should the good Mayor's letters cease we will be hunting for you and your company, Master Hopkins." Hopkins seethed. His eyes narrowed to a squint. "What is the name of the cursed woman of whom you speak?"

"Ellie. Ellie Harewood," came a voice from within the crowd. Ted made his way to the front of the people watching the scene unfold, his face battered, aged and marked by despair and sadness. "He took my only daughter from me last night, and bound her to a tree," he snarled towards Hopkins.

"Then it is Ellie Harewood whom the King expects to be delivered. It can be no-one other than her, Mayor, do you understand?"

"Indeed I do."

"Very good." The soldier made way back to his company. The Witchfinder General watched as he jumped back in to the saddle. "The King expects you in London in a month's time with the body of the accused Ellie Harewood, to be examined for symptoms of witchcraft. Should you fail to deliver this woman, both you and your company will be hauled in front of the esteemed Sir John Bankes, Chief Justice of the Common Pleas, to face charges of perjury and fraud, both of which carry the death penalty if found to be guilty."

Hopkins stunned at the charges. "Ellie Harewood. One month in London. Do not interfere with the correspondence. Do not dare haul a different body to London in her place. Should anything be tampered with you will face further charges and will be trialled accordingly. Good day to you gentlemen, and good luck. May God protect you all."

The soldiers left Elkwood. Normality returned to all except the Witchfinder and his company. "What now?" Stearne asked. His anger was apparent.

"I don't believe the King would interfere in our work, Stearne."

"He does know about it, doesn't he?"

Hopkins turned to his companion. "Of course! Don't question me or my authority!" Turning from his comrade he looked about the town and noticed Randall, Reverend Thomas and the treasurer watching them from the boundary of the Mayor's home. Mian smiled. Hopkins turned away in disgust. "Let's cut her body down and begin the journey to London, today," he ordered, as the town's people went about their business. "I want this over with as soon as possible."

"Of course. I'll get the men on it right away."

Hopkins watched as his company entered the trees and made their way toward the body of Ellie in the clearing. He thought this would be a simple task.

Belief

Darkness faded into light. Light dwindled back to darkness. Consciousness came. Consciousness diminished. Sweet, fresh smells were sensed. The sound of liquid bubbling emerged and diminished. Ellie trembled whenever she became conscious, shivering as her body thawed. Voices became audible as she drifted in and out, in and out. She felt like death.

"...fingers and toes?"

"Frozen solid. Only the brew will return them..."

Darkness.

"...is working. Keep her covered."

The sound of the bubbling liquid drifted to her from a distance. A gentle breeze skewered pain through her side as it caressed the skin.

"...like nothing ever before. She must survive. Her..."

Ellie emerged from the slumber, aware of certain voices and sensations she had felt during her drift between consciousness. She lay beneath a vast heap of animal furs. Above, small tree trunks pushed close together to support a flimsy looking shelter from which foliage occasionally fell. A cauldron sat inside a fire pit, excavated in the floor beside her. The room was surprisingly large and the heat from the fire beneath the pot was welcome against her cool skin. The cauldron placed in the middle of the room which had only a small, rickety door in the timber walls for exit. Dead animals and their appendages hung from twine stretched between the walls. Body parts ranging from rabbit's feet to bats wings hung there. Ellie sat upright, rubbing her eyes. She drew her hands away and noticed black fingertips. Touching them, they felt normal; there was no pain or discomfort. She remembered the tingling, stabbing sensation during the harsh night and wondered if that had been the sign they had frozen.

The room was otherwise empty. The only life besides her was the cauldron boiling. Ellie decided to stand, feeling slightly nauseous the more upright she became. Her cotton dress hung from the rafters. Reaching down Ellie grabbed the largest of the furs and quickly wrapped it around her naked body. Intrigued by the surroundings she explored, finding numerous dirty glass jars containing liquids of various colours and more body parts. One in particular drew her attention. She reached out and grabbed it, drawing it closer. Pupils of varying size stared back, crammed in their hundreds from inside the preserve. "What are these?"

"Eyes of newt."

Ellie jumped and placed the jar back, quickly turning to see who had spoken. On the other side of the cauldron stood a grotesque, hunched hag. A prominent chin and even larger nose hooked downward, its tip almost reaching a wrinkled lip. Skin drew over bone; her face gaunt, almost lifeless. Ellie recalled the hooded figure that approached in her hour of need. "Who are you?" she asked, clutching the fur to her body.

The hag shuffled awkwardly around the cauldron. Ellie kept a firm gaze upon her as she approached.

"I am the one who rescued you from the very clutches of death. I arrived to you before he did and saved your soul, for the time being."

Ellie was confused. She recalled something like this being said when she was roped to the tree.

"I see you be feeling better. Up on your feet now?"

"Answer me. Who are you?" Ellie snapped, more from nervousness than anger.

"My dear, do not demand in such a manner to someone who saved your life as I did." The hag stooped down unsteadily and picked up a wooden ladle from the floor. She reached through the steam of the cauldron, placed the utensil in to the liquid, stirred the waters and withdrew. "You'll need to take this," she said, holding the ladle towards Ellie.

Ellie scrunched her face in disgust. "What is it?"

"A potion you have been taking between your slumbers."

Ellie's look went from one of disgust to confusion. "How long have I been sleeping?"

"One day, and already you are behind."

"Behind what?"

"Here, child, it will not harm you. It will replace your energy."

After a moment's hesitation Ellie reached out and took the ladle. She peered down to see nothing more than a clear liquid, like water. After studying it a while longer she looked up at her host. The hag gestured upwards with an open palm. Ellie took one last look and put the ladle to her lips, blowing on it gently to cool the concoction. After a brief hesitation she swallowed the liquid in one gulp. Tasteless but hot, it burned down in to her stomach. Ellie frowned at the sensation, handed the utensil back to the hag, placed a fist over her mouth and coughed.

"There we are," the hag replied, "it should be your last. It will force the ice from your body and replenish your reserves. Come, sit down." Her host offered a hand out towards a wooden chair across the room. "I'll tell you everything."

Ellie reluctantly complied, clutching the fur closer as she moved round the cauldron. Soon she rested on the furniture, bathing in the heat from the fire. The hag pottered about for a moment or so, taking two wooden mugs from the recesses of the room. Ellie watched as she sprinkled them with a substance from another pot and added hot water from the cauldron.

"Here." Ellie took the mug offered and studied the steaming darkness within.

"What is it?" she asked, noticing dark blotches floating on the surface.

"A mixture of herbs picked from the forest around us." Ellie blew on the liquid once more and took a gentle sip. The drink was aromatic, fragrant and took her by surprise.

"Very good, isn't it?" The hag smiled. Ellie nodded slowly as she took another sip. The hag sipped her own. "To think, acting in such a way would have us accused of witchcraft." Ellie looked to the host. The hag watched from the rim of her mug. "I know. It was these very herbs I was collecting at dawn yesterday when I stumbled across you, bound to that tree, frozen through and almost dead." Ellie looked about the room, interpreting an accusation. "Be not threatened, child, I am here to help you."

"How? Why would you save someone accused of witchcraft?"

The hag smiled and placed her mug on the floor. Opening her palms she released two butterflies. Ellie marvelled as they floated around the room, their paths sparkling as they fluttered through the air. She watched as the brightly coloured insects rose to the rafters of the room and vanished in the shadows. "How did you…" But a memory jogged in the back of her mind. This was the one of whom the townspeople talked, the one on whom they blamed their misfortunes. Ellie became fearful.

"Do not be afraid, my dear, I mean you no harm."

"But you're…"

"Yes, I'm the one of which your town's population speaks, but you need not be afraid of me. I am here to help you. Let me explain."

"No!" Ellie snapped, rising from her seat. She hurried over to the dress, grabbed it and noted how cold and wet the cotton had remained. It would have to do.

"Let me explain," the hag began, watching from across the cauldron.

"You're a witch, and a threat."

"And you're not?"

Ellie stopped, gazing in to the shadows of the room. "No, they just think I am." She pulled the dress over and shivered at its damp coldness.

"Where will you go? You can't return to Elkwood, they'll kill you for certain."

"I don't know," Ellie sighed as she considered what she could do. The hag was right, there was nowhere to go.

"Whether you believe me or no, you do have an immense power to become an unstoppable being. You just do not realise it."

"I am not a witch."

"But you are," the hag whispered in a sinister voice, "and one to be feared."

Ellie stopped again and looked down, considering what the woman said. "I am not," she repeated once more, "I am just a woman, no greater or worse than the next." Ellie headed to the door.

"Do not leave!" the hag ordered. "If you leave my care you will succumb to death!"

"She's right." Both women turned to the area where Ellie had been sleeping as Samael appeared from the shadows. "The only reason you still live is because Sister Luna here bartered with me on your behalf. You leave that door against her wishes and you leave with me on a journey to the other side."

"If you leave now you will die," Luna echoed.

Samael emerged in to the room. "Watch," he said, holding out his palm. From the rafters the two butterflies that Luna had conjured slowly fluttered from their hiding place, headed towards his open hand. As they reached his palm their brightly coloured wings crumbled to powder, leaving nothing more than their skeletons. "See." He gently blew on their remains. Both turned to dust and scattered in to the air. Samael adjusted his top hat. "Ellie, you owe this lady your life. You have much to do unless you want me to take yours instead."

"I made a bargain with him on your behalf," Luna explained, "and if you don't see it through, your life will be taken as it should have been when I found you bound to the tree."

"The truth is, Ellie, you're a witch. Whether you believe us both or not is your decision. You do, however, have two options. One, you can leave through that door and your feet won't even touch the frozen mud outside. You'll be travelling with me to the spirit world where I may use you to barter for my own personal gain, something of which you'll have no control whatsoever. Or, number two, you can listen to us both, realise that there's something more to yourself than you actually believe, whether you like it or not, fulfil your end of the bargain and we can all live happily thereafter. It's your choice now, Ellie. Your life hinges on this decision. It's up to you."

Luna shuffled closer. "Think of the hurt your townspeople caused you. Think of the anger and hatred you felt for them as they judged and sentenced you to death. Remember that they wanted you dead. Even your own father and your only love did nothing to assist you."

Ellie saw the face of her father, of whom had done nothing as she was manhandled from the town. Anger began to emerge, much like it had done at that time.

Luna rested a hand on her arm. "I felt the power that lays dormant within you, Ellie. I know how powerful your potential is. You can become feared amongst the people of this country, and in turn live in fear of no-one."

"The power that lies within you is the only thing which you can use to deliver me the souls you've promised," Samael told her.

"What souls?" Ellie asked, her gaze flicking between the two.

"In order for you to live I had to barter something that Samael would find attractive. You must deliver fifty souls to him by the end of the full moon next month, or both you and I will lose our lives in payment."

"What?" Ellie whispered. The whole situation was far too much for her to comprehend.

Ellie turned to Samael, who brushed his fingernails across the chest of his coat. "Fifty souls, Ellie, all delivered by *your* hand." He pointed to her. "If not, both you and Sister Luna can expect to be holding this conversation somewhere on the other side. And it will be all your own doing. It's your choice, Ellie. Leave now and die, or stay with Sister Luna, let her help realise your powers and give yourself a chance to live. One choice Ellie, that is all you have." Samael turned to Luna. "I will return at dawn tomorrow if Ellie still rejects the proposal you made in her place." He then turned back to Ellie and fumbled with the red sash across his waist. "Dawn, Ellie. If by then you have yet to accept the terms of your bargain you will die."

Ellie didn't believe fully in either of these testimonies, but witnessing the butterflies emerging from Luna's palms and then crumbling upon Samael's skin was very convincing. Remembering how it felt as the freezing temperatures had took hold in the forest, there had only been a matter of minutes between life and death. She remembered how the elements attacked, and unless she wanted to pass into the spirit world, the only hope was to take the guidance of this dishevelled old woman offering her sanctuary. Whether he was a mystical being as he purported, or some kind of murderous magician, there was no way either of these people would allow her live against their terms. She turned to face Samael.

"He has gone," Luna explained as Ellie looked about the room. "You have now to make your choice. Do you stand with me and believe in the ability which lay dormant inside you, or do you spend your last night in this existence worrying about the fate that arrives with the morning sun?"

Ellie returned her focus to Luna. "If I agree to stay with you, what must I do?"

"Have belief in yourself, Ellie, nothing more. The existence in which we live is not as simple as you have been led to believe. Believe in that which is around you, in the things you will learn, and you will soon become confident in yourself and you're ability. When you reach that level of thinking, there will be no way you can be stopped."

Ellie thought things over a moment, recalling the house trembling as she awoke from a nightmare. "What will I be capable of?"

Luna smiled. "Whatever you can imagine."

Anxiety

Hopkins paced around the Mayor's lounge with increasing distress. "What do you mean she wasn't there?" His frustration increased with each statement relayed back by his company. "She would simply not just vanished!"

"Master Hopkins, she was not there!" Stearne snapped, running a hand through his dark beard. Hopkins could see the anxiety of his oldest comrade appear through expression.

"The ropes were still bound as we had left them," Lucian began, "but she had gone. We explored the area but she was not there."

"It was as though she had just fallen through the ropes," Daniel added.

Randall and Mian studied the Witchfinder General as his anger deepened. Had he looked at that precise moment, Hopkins would notice Mian smiling, undoubtedly toward his predicament.

"There is not a single chance she would have fallen through the ropes!" he shouted, coming to rest in front of the fire. "It can be one of two things. One, she was rescued by someone, or two, you fools were not competent to undertake that for which I pay you so handsomely."

Lucian drew his rapier and prodded its tip against the throat of the Witchfinder. "I pray, sir, that you did not intend offending us or our work, as it was I and my good friend John who bound her to that tree. If my work were to be questioned I may be angered and act accordingly."

Hopkins lifted a gloved hand and moved the rapier to one side. "If she was bound as strongly as you say, then it means only one thing." Lucian nodded and lowered the blade. Hopkins turned toward the town dignitaries. "It would seem that your young witch is stronger than I imagined."

Mian beamed. "Indeed she is. Perhaps now you will earn your money."

"Indeed." Hopkins turned away and peered through the window in to the town. "We may be here a while longer."

Mind

Ellie basked within the warmth of a monstrous fire created outside the small, foliage built lodging in which Sister Luna dwelled. The new shawl which Luna had given felt snug and kept the cold at bay, and the log upon she sat was not as uncomfortable as initially perceived.

"They will be with us soon," the old hag muttered as she lurched down beside Ellie.

Ellie had become apprehensive since Luna explained they were not alone in this part of the forest. she mentioned nothing else about these people; only that they would visit that very night, and that it be extremely important.

Ellie accepted her fate with Sister Luna, and having seen Samael's power, became more at ease with the grotesque hag into whose care she was assigned.

The fire crackled and popped.

"Do not fret, child, you are welcome here, and you are safe."

Ellie flashed a smile. Life was changing dramatically, for better or worse could not be told, and the new direction she was heading appeared mysterious and unknown.

"Luna," she said gently, her gaze mesmerised by the fire, "do you really think I have power?"

Sister Luna burst in to a cackle and reached over, patting Ellie's thigh. "My dear, I would not have bartered my very life if I was at all unsure. You do possess our powers, Ellie, and as soon as we can unlock your mind and have you believing the same, the better."

"Are there many of you? Witches I mean?"

"Us, Ellie. Are there many of us, you mean." Luna leant closer. "There are, scattered here and there across the country. Some are very evil, making human sacrifice in our Lord's name. I do not carry out such practices myself, I never needed to. But there are indeed some hideously evil beings out there."

Ellie's mind returned to the imminent arrival of their guests. "Will the people we are meeting help us?"

Luna withdrew her hand and placed her palms toward the amber flames. "Yes, and no," she replied, rubbing them together. "They will help us in our hour of need, but to unlock your mind, I'm afraid only you can do that. With my help, of course."

"How will they help? What will they do?"

"In time, Ellie, in time. First, you must become one with yourself and your mind." Luna placed her hands in her lap. "Shall we begin?" Ellie shifted her gaze to the hag and said nothing. "This is the beginning, Ellie, this moment, this night. There is no turning back from here on in. You will realise your potential or we shall both be doomed. This is the time. It is now that we will begin. Are you ready?"

Nervousness fluttered in Ellie's stomach. Now or never. Now was the time. She didn't understand what she was to do, but felt at ease with Sister Luna and trusted her completely. "I'm ready," she whispered.

Luna turned to the flames. "Look into the fire, Ellie, and tell me what you see. Look deep, beyond the curtains of the flames, and tell me what meet's your eye in its deepest recess." Ellie held a breath. "Open your mind, not your eyes." She focused on a part of the fire glowing yellow inside its base. "Feel your restrictions vanishing, Ellie. Feel your mind open. Embrace it. Realise your potential." The flames entranced her. "With an open mind comes an open existence. Your restrictions vanish. There is no barrier to hold you there. Free yourself. Release your inner self. Call to your subconscious. Draw it forward. Call its power." The forest swayed up and down, left and right, round and round. Ellie struggled to remain conscious. "Almost there, Ellie. Feel the power emerging." A warm, peaceful sensation smothered Ellie, welcome and unlike any she had known before.

"Now, see the flames, imagine them roaring high in to the sky, past the trees and up in to the heavens. Imagine it, Ellie, create it." The sensation became more intense. It surged. "Feel it. See it. The flames." Ellie saw the flames in her mind's eye, the same that haunted her dreams, orange, red, but more intense.

The fire exploded into the sky, shaking the ground. Ellie fell back, legs upright as she thudded to the ground. A brief shake of the head returned reality, and with it the vision of Luna looking down from the log. She smiled. Ellie looked around, shocked and confused, and noticed two people sitting opposite. A man dressed in simple clothing smiled. He had thick stubble and jet black hair. A woman accompanied him, dressed as simply as he.

"You're right, Sister, I believe she may be the one you've waited for," the dark haired man said from across the flames. Luna patted the bark where Ellie had been sitting. Now embarrassed, Ellie stood, brushed the leaves from the cloak and sat on the natural seat beside Luna.

"Ellie, I would like you to meet Wagner." The man with the dark stubble nodded to her. "And this is his daughter, Agnieszka."

"The last time I saw you, you were bound to a tree and close to death," Wagner stated, his voice tinged with a strange accent from across the seas.

"Wagner carried you back here," Luna explained as they sat in the warmth of the fire. "He brought you to my home where I nursed you back from the cold. You have much to thank him for."

Ellie looked across. From his chiselled features he did not appear to be of these lands, and could not place the accent with which he spoke. She dropped her head. "Thank you." Wagner waved a hand as though bowing in response.

Luna took charge of the meeting. "Now, we must start your training, Ellie. We must see where to begin."

Wagner nodded. "We can help. We work in league with Sister Luna. There are many things we can assist with."

"Are you witches as well?" Ellie enquired, shivering at the cold air the warmth of the flames could not reach.

"Indeed not, we have, you might say, different qualities."

"Lycanthropes," Luna whispered.

"Werewolves?"

"Werewolves, lycanthropes, they are one and the same. And we are them," Agnieszka answered in Luna's place.

Luna prodded the fire with a stick. "You have nothing to fear, what you know of lycanthropes and of witches comes from the opinions of your townspeople. People fear what they do not understand, just as they feared you, enough to execute you out here in the forest."

"I had done nothing to harm any of them," Ellie replied. Sorrow took her heart for a moment as she remembered how callously the townspeople had treated her. "Yet, they still judged me. They decided to take my life based on that simple belief. Someone shouted 'witch' and they judged me."

Luna sighed. "But why, Ellie? Why would they do that? From what I understand you made structures quake in their foundations."

Ellie gripped her shawl. "How did you know that?"

Luna laughed. "My dear, being a witch has its advantages. You will learn about the spies of the forest in time. First, we must concentrate on you. The fact that your mind created such an event in your town reveals the potential of your power. You possess a power greater than any that has walked the earth before you, and we must find a way to help you unlock it."

"But how? How can you unlock something that may not even be there?"

"The power of belief, my dear, the power of belief. You saw how high the flames exploded when you willed it to happen? That was of your own creation. Believing in that will be a start."

"Ellie, you do have the power. All you need do is believe in yourself," Wagner added.

"But what is it? Where does it come from?" she asked, struggling to believe that a power as great as they believed could go un-noticed . With many questions and few answers she was became confused.

"Witchcraft is an age old power," Luna began, shuffling on the log as though to make herself more comfortable. "It is as old as the stars themselves. We call it power, but it is more a skill than anything else. It dwells deep within the human mind, and for those powerful enough to harness its full potential it will allow them to create anything it may conjure." Luna held a palm out to the fire. A flame jumped and ignited her hand. Ellie jumped. "Fret not, child, but learn." She held the flaming hand toward her pupil, opened her fingers and gently waved the flame. "Do you see this?"

Ellie nodded. "Yes," she replied, amazed that the fire burned on Luna's skin.

"You can feel the heat with which it burns, too. This flame is as strong and potent as any of its kind, yet it succumbs to my command merely by thought and suggestion. Your mind can create anything it so desires, just as I have done. By simply wanting this flame I can manipulate it to feast upon my skin without fear of injury. I can bend it to my own will in a way that few others can." Ellie watched, mesmerised by the teachings of the hag. "If you so desire to have this flame, Ellie, you can, but you must believe in what you see, and believe in yourself. Here, take it from me."

Ellie's eyes widened. "Take it? What, me?"

"You have so little time to master this art my child, and you must learn quickly, for your very life depends on it. Believe that this fire will not harm you. Believe that it will fuel itself from your hand. You must take it and feel the power you possess. Here." Luna gestured with the flame. "Hurry now, Ellie."

"Believe," Wagner chanted as the lycanthropes watched from beyond the campfire.

Ellie returned the gaze to Luna's palm, her heart pounding. The flame tormented and teased as it flickered from the fingers of its mistress. Ellie sighed long and hard, attempting to convince herself she believed in what this strange guild were preaching. She could possess this power. She could own this flame. Carefully her palm reached toward to Luna's. Luna grabbed her wrist and squeezed tight.

"Remember your power!" she snapped angrily. Ellie watched as the flame leapt from Luna and burned upon her own skin. She screamed and yanked away from Luna's clutch, to no avail. Luna stared maniacally at her. "My fate rests in your palms, Ellie, never forget that! Believe in yourself and save us both from the consequence of death!" She threw Ellie's hand away. The clearing fell silent. The tranquil peace of the wilderness returned. Ellie had been caught off guard by her mentor, and the shock of the incident left tears burning at the back of her eyes. Luna's complexion had changed momentarily to one of malevolence and rage, and the intensity she had displayed was frightening. Although the flame hadn't been on her hand long enough to do damage she noticed the gentle sensation of warmth where it had been in contact. Wagner and Agnieszka looked on from their place across the flames separating them both from the witches. Gradually regaining composure, Ellie noticed something. Something so amazing that her mouth dropped in astonishment. Her left index finger was flickering with a small flame. It danced as any fire would do; only this one burned at the end of her fingertip. Through the flame Ellie saw the skin had not blistered or broken, and watched on with wonder as it continued to burn. "There," Luna said, her voice returning to the calm tone to which Ellie had been accustomed, "let this be your first lesson in witchcraft. Believe in yourself."

Ellie waved the flame and smiled. "I am controlling this?" she asked, now unaware of how cold the night around her had become.

"Experiment," Luna suggested. "Use your imagination." Ellie frowned, unable to comprehend what was happening, but willing to believe in what she saw. Slowly the fire levitated into the air. The flame ascended further before a passing breeze extinguished her creation. A small hiccup of laughter expelled from her mouth, more from excitement than any other emotion. "You are on the right path," Luna congratulated her. Ellie's first spell had been cast. Samael would not be needed for now. Her training had begun.

Signs

Hopkins dismounted from his horse in the frosty, clear, dawn. The air bit harshly in the crimson skies as the winter sun slowly emerged. Lucian and Stearne dropped to the freezing ground and accompanied Hopkins through the opening, towards the tree where Ellie had been bound. Reverend Williams, the expert in demonology and Daniel Wade, the company marksman, stood while the rest of hunters investigated the area. Forests were treacherous places at the best of times, but dawn and twilight were particularly menacing. Many strange occurrences happened during these hours.

The three men wandered across the frozen grounds as they approached the contorted tree. Across the open behind them Wade's horse snorted. A bird fluttered within the branches, its wings battering the limbs as it escaped into the morning sky. Hopkins stared at the tree for an age, struggling to find a rational explanation for how the witch escaped her fate. He noticed Stearne shiver in the cold air, then looked across to Lucian who had begun investigating the clearing. "It seems you were indeed correct. This is bound solidly to the tree." Removing one of his gloves he attempted take hold of the rope. There was no room to place his fingers behind, it had been pulled too tightly. His breath clouded into the morning air.

"Look here." Hopkins turned to Lucian. The hunter dropped to one knee and investigated the terrain.

"What have you found?" he asked, peering over Lucian's shoulder.

Lucian began indicating marks on the ground. "She wasn't alone." he pointed to Hopkins a disturbance to the frozen grass where a patch of leaves had been flattened. "This is a print. A small one, but still a print. This one over here is of similar size, and made by the opposite foot, but it is lighter. Whoever these belong to walks unsteadily, and was heavier on one foot than the other."

Hopkins stared at the tracks, attempting to make sense of what he was seeing. "What direction did they come from?" Lucian failed to respond. Stearne slapped his arms to generate some heat, distracting Hopkins as he allowed the tracker time for composure.

"Over there," Lucian finally replied, pointing to the north-west where the trees became closer, and where it was much, much darker.

Stearne stomped his feet. "It's been over a day since we were here last. Could those tracks have been made since?"

Lucian turned to him and nodded. "It's possible, but unlikely I would feel. The people of the town fear this forest and would dare not venture this far individually, believing these woods cursed by werewolves and witches."

Hopkins nodded. "Indeed. They are a simple folk, and simple folk have simple fears. I doubt very much that any one of those peasants would dare journey out here, and at least not without our knowing. Word travels fast in that town and we most certainly would have been alerted should anyone have contemplated doing so."

"What should our next move involve, then?" Stearne asked the company leader.

Hopkins glanced over his shoulder and gave a brief smile. "We do what we do best, Master Stearne. We follow the track as far as we possibly can and reclaim our witch. Do the tracks return to the darkened forest?" he then asked, shifting his gaze to Lucian.

"I believe so, but the second tracks, those I presume belong to our Miss Harewood, look much heavier than what the wench could create. The uneven prints continue beside them, indicating two people, but I am concerned as to the depth and stride of this second set. I take it our witch was not too heavy to drag here?" he then asked, this time looking to Stearne.

"Not at all. She was as light as a feather."

"Then there were two people with her," Hopkins mused, "the person who made these uneven prints and one with a heavier mass."

Lucian adjusted his scarf. "Yes, that is what I believe from studying these tracks. She received assistance from someone, of that I'm sure. The presence of two tracks suggest she was carried by the person making the larger prints. She has had help."

Hopkins stared at the trees. "The one they spoke of," he said quietly as he gazed in to the distance. "The hag. Margaret Addler. The one they accused of cursing their lands."

"The one that stopped the trade routes to their town," Stearne recalled. Lucian pushed himself to his feet and brushed condensation from his hands.

"The very one," Hopkins confirmed.

"And the lycanthropes," Lucian added.

Hopkins smiled his malicious smile. "It makes perfect sense."

"Two witches? Werewolves?" Stearne asked.

"No one said this was going to be an easy task," Hopkins replied. "Do you know what's at stake here?"

"Indeed I do."

"Then we must not hesitate a second more. We begin by following this trail. Let us first find where it leads. To a simple dwelling of some sort I would presume, and then we plan our move."

Familiars

Ellie awoke to the familiar noise of the bubbling cauldron. She slept in the same spot beneath the same furs. The heat from the fire bathed the room with warmth, banishing the cold outside the dwelling. She stirred and sat upright. Luna hobbled over, clasping a mug. "Good morning my dear," she said jovially, handing it across to the young woman. "Drink this. It will warm your bones and prepare you for the long day ahead." Ellie took the mug and drank the liquid before handing it back without uttering a word. "You have some visitors," Luna told her, a smile on her contorted features.

Ellie squirmed nervously. "Who would be looking for me?"

"Do not fear," the hag replied as she moved away. From behind her cloak emerged a red fox. It stood proud, appearing unafraid and confident. Around its left eye, a dash of white fur streaked through the red, from top to bottom.

Ellie frowned. "A fox?"

"Not just a fox," Luna explained, looking up to the rafters. A bright barn owl perched upon a beam and peered down toward her.

"Summon the fox," Luna ordered.

"How? It's a wild animal."

"Indeed he is, but I think there's something more to these creatures than you may consider. Try it."

Ellie stared toward the fox. It stood there, unflinching, looking directly back to her. She reached out and turned her palm upright. The fox continued to stare. She opened her fingers. "Here," Ellie said softly. Warily the fox walked toward her, and within a moment rubbed the side of his muzzle in her palm. An image of the hand flashed within her mind, jolting Ellie as it appeared. The fox lifted his muzzle. Ellie's saw her own face appear in her mind, revealing her sleepy expression.

"Your eyes and ears, my dear," Luna stated, noticing that Ellie was nervous.

"What's happening?"

"It's the bond you share. We all have animals that help us hear and see things we would otherwise miss."

"Spies?"

"Familiars, my dear, every witch will have them. These creature will help you in your quests." Ellie reached out and petted the fox. It curled in and sat on the furs she was nestled beneath.

"Hold out your arm." Luna glanced up at the barn owl perched in the rafters. The owl's head turned sideways as if studying Ellie as she looked to him. "Won't his talons cut me?"

"He is your servant, dear. He will not harm his mistress. Call to him."

Ellie lifted her elbow and forearm. With a beat of his wings the owl glided down and rested on her arm, and, just as Luna had said, perched there gently without clenching its talons or drawing blood. Ellie surveyed the room from the owl's perspective, just as she had done with the fox. "Amazing." She marvelled at the creatures.

"Indeed it is, Ellie. They will stay with you through thick and thin, for better or for worse. Nothing is greater than the bond between a witch and her Familiars."

"Will they face any danger?"

"Only if they are discovered to be assisting you. Most times they are dismissed as simple woodland animals. When they are not needed they will remain safe, somewhere near to where you live, which for the time being will be here with me. You can summon them whenever you so require, and they will answer."

"And how do I do that?"

"By using your mind, my dear. Think of them and call to them. You must give both creatures a name, though. They must know they are being summoned."

"Will they know the names that I give?"

"Of course they will. They know that you are their mistress."

"But what to call them?" Ellie pondered. The owl grew heavy on her arm. He was bright and pristine, with dark eyes that stood vibrantly against his heart shaped face. "You look so wise and intelligent." The owl ruffled his wings. Then it came to her. "Cyrius." The owl hooted and launched itself back to the rafters. "And as for you," she added, looking down to the fox, "there's only one name I can give to you with that white fur running through your eye. I think you should be named Streak."

"Wise names, my dear, and unique too. They will not confuse you." Luna moved across to the door of the dwelling. "Now, be gone with you, your mistress has a busy day. Return when you are called." Cyrius swooped down and out in to the chilly morning. Streak turned and dashed through the open door leaving pupil and mentor in each other's company.

"Do you have Familiars?" Ellie asked as Luna returned to her chair.

Luna cackled. "Indeed I do, Ellie, indeed I do, but you must never, ever reveal the identities of your Familiars to anyone. Should word get back to Elkwood or the witch-hunting community, you would place both yourself and your animals at great risk. Never disclose their identities to anyone, never. Now, my dear, today is where your training really begins."

Oddity

Matthew Hopkins led his company along a trail between birch trees and ferns. The ferns were so dense in this part of the forest that it was hard to detect the earth of the trail as they journeyed on deeper between the trees. Lucian followed the tracks on to the natural pathway but lost them as they merged with the contours of the trail. It was impossible to see where the tracks he'd been following were leading, and then, they vanished. With ferns this dense inside the forest the prints could, and probably did, leave the trail and Lucian would remain none the wiser.

"This is going to be like looking for a needle in a haystack," Stearne muttered. He swayed from side to side as his horse trotted between the greenery.

"Indeed it is, Master Stearne, but we must remain optimistic," Hopkins replied, himself appearing happier than he had been since their journey began. "I do not wish to stand trial in front of our King, what say you?"

"No sir, not at all."

Hopkins knew there was no possible way they could prove their success without a witch on display, but even then he wondered how the royal physicians could confirm or deny that a woman was a witch.

After a while Hopkins raised a hand to his company and brought the steeds to a standstill. "Stop." The horses snorted.

"What is it? What's the matter?" Stearne asked.

"Up there, ahead." Hopkins pointed. A naked body knelt across the carcass of a fallow deer. The body's spine protruded beneath tight, pale skin. It bore dirty feet, probably from wandering the forest unshod. The company watched as the hunched body tore at the animal and ate flesh from the carcass.

"Master Wade." Hopkins summoned the archer, frowning in disgust at the oddity. Hopkins heard the crossbow draw from Daniel's shoulder and knew it was aimed toward the beast. The creature lifted its bald head. Hopkins noticed its protruding ears. "Father, come here please." Reverend Williams appeared by his side. The creature turned and studied the company with white, lifeless eyes. Its nose hooked downward and pointed at the tip. The lower half its face was hidden by blood. "Pray tell?" Hopkins asked, pointing at the creature smothered in gore.

"It is nothing more than a half-blood, sir," Williams explained.

"A half-blood of what?" Both watched as the grotesque creature turned its attention back to the deer and delved deeper in to the depths of the animal's body.

"A hybrid of species. Nosferatu and human."

"Nosferatu?" Hopkins had never dealt with vampires during daylight hours when applying his trade.

"Indeed. Usually a human will be turned by a single bite of the night crawlers. They carry the ability to pass the curse through this simple means. They kill whomever they feast upon but on occasion will turn a human to vampire form."

"And is this the result?" Hopkins asked with disgust, waving a gloved hand at the creature blocking their path.

"No, this is the result of a partial turn. This is done to punish troublesome humans or to create simple assistants. I would imagine this creature has a master to whom it will answer."

"If it is indeed a vampire, why is it not destroyed in the daylight?" Stearne asked.

"Because it's only half-blood," Williams explained. "It can exist in dull light. The thick cover that the forest provides in this part limits any daylight that penetrates to the ground, even in the height of the summer." The half-blood lifted its head from the gutted deer and stumbled slowly to its feet, turning to face its watchers. Each studied the other in silence. The branches rustled about them in the gentle breeze. Slowly the hybrid began moving. One shoulder drooped, with a limp arm that swayed as it moved.

"We don't often receive visitors this deep in the forest," the half-blood snarled in a high pitched voice. Hopkins' horse snorted as the creature approached.

"What a fine animal, very fine indeed."

"That is close enough, if you please," Hopkins asked authoritatively.

The half-blood stopped and nodded. "Of course, of course." It rubbed its long fingers around its mouth. "But I must ask what it is that brings you noble gentlemen so deep within this cursed forest?"

"We are looking for a young woman, a witch, who we believe may be lurking in this area."

"A witch you say? There is but one that I know who lives within this forest, and you are way from her territory."

"The hag?" Stearne suggested to his comrades.

"Indeed." Hopkins turned back to the blood-soaked creature. "Tell me, do you know where we might find this witch with whom you are familiar?"

"I do my very best to avoid her. She can be found east of here, living in harmony with those who howl by the moon."

"It is as I thought." The hybrid began panting nervously. "What troubles you?" Hopkins asked the creature, noticing its distress.

"Take it away! Take it away!" it growled, flapping towards the clergyman. "Go! Go now! Leave me in peace!"

Hopkins frowned. "We will go when…"

The half-blood launched to Williams. A whistle cut the air as it slumped to the ground, a single arrow protruding above its left brow. The company of men looked back to Daniel who placed the crossbow across his back. Hopkins nodded his approval and Williams nodded in thanks. The clergyman wiped the creature's blood from his skin with the edge of a cape. Hopkins swayed as his horse moved upon the uneven ground, and looked to the east as the half-blood had instructed.

Stearne wiped a spot of blood on to his sleeve. "What now? It will be too difficult to navigate through the forest from here, to be sure. It's too dense."

"Then we take a different approach," Hopkins explained, quietly despairing at Stearne's single-mindedness.

"What do you have in mind?"

Hopkins smiled upon hatching a despicable idea. "Bait, Master Stearne. We use live bait."

Patience

In Elkwood, the day drew on. The cold sunshine turned to twilight, prompting the townsfolk to retreat to their homes or to the tavern. Mayor Randall walked through his township with Reverend Thomas. Both had been distressed by the recent events befalling their community, and even more so now that Matthew Hopkins and his company would be taking residence for longer than anticipated. The Witchfinder's behaviour and his methods had made everyone uneasy.

The two made their way through the small buildings to Randall's residence across the square.

"What do you think will happen?" Reverend Thomas asked.

"I do not know!" Randall snapped, angry that for once he could not rectify the problems his town experienced.

Thomas appeared upset by the response. Randall noticed and adjusted his tone. "There's no saying what they'll do in the name of the King. We must simply hope they find the Harewood girl and leave for London by dawn's early light, leaving our township in peace."

"Ah, the very gentleman," echoed a familiar voice from the darkness. Randall looked through the fading light to see five shadows emerging into the square. At the head of them was Hopkins, a demonic smile strewn upon his face. "Your servants informed me you were patrolling your town."

"Master Hopkins," Randall began, hiding his dismay that the Witchfinder had returned, "did luck serve you well in your quest for Miss Harewood?"

Hopkins sighed, rolling his eyes. "Alas my good man it did not. I am the bearer of bad tidings I am afraid."

"May I ask what they may be?" Thomas asked.

"Indeed sir, you may. It would appear that young Miss Harewood has escaped from the tree to which she was bound."

"Good lord," Randall whispered.

"Now fret not, Master Randall, she is not beyond apprehension," Hopkins assured him.

"But how? The forest is so dense and so vast that you may never find her."

"Indeed we will. The bad news we bring is also somewhat encouraging."

"And how may that be?" the Reverend asked.

Hopkins placed his arm around the Mayor and gestured for them all to walk. The company of men followed his lead and walked within the darkness across the square. "We found that she was helped to escape by some other person, one whose tracks lead right here to Elkwood."

"What?" Randall shouted, turning to the Witchfinder.

"Indeed it is true. My esteemed companion, Lucian, found the prints leading to the very outskirts of your township."

Randall looked at the hunter. "Do you know who it was?"

"Indeed we do."

"Her father?" Thomas asked.

"No. Although grieving for his daughter, he did not return to the trees to assist her."

"Oh no..." Randall exhaled as realisation set in. Momentarily, Hopkins clasped him tighter. "Unfortunately, yes. Young love is a powerful emotion, Master Randall, and one as smitten as he would be easily influenced by one such as her."

They walked in silence for a moment. "Then what do you suggest we do?" the Reverend asked.

Hopkins slapped Randall's back. "Assisting a witch in any way is crime punishable by death, and this is what must be applied."

"But to one as young as he?" the Mayor asked.

"Unfortunately so. The younger they are, the more influenced they become. If simply left to go about his business he will soon fall to her power. We must strike now."

"Poor lad," Thomas whispered.

"Allow us to take him and deliver to the Lord graciously. We will go far from the community to lessen the distress to your town, and we will take his life in a dignified way."

Randall looked to the Witchfinder. "Do we even have a choice? Will you not tell us that it is the Lord's work you are completing, being carried out in the King's good name?"

Hopkins stopped, presenting an expression of confusion. "I pray for your apology, good sir. By what did you mean by that statement?"

Randall walked to the head of the company and turned to face them. "Is it not your business to kill anyone and everyone accused of witchcraft? You will do whatever is needed. I am concerned, Master Hopkins, concerned that my letter to Parliament addressed our troubles with the hag who haunts these very surroundings, and yet you choose to trial the younger, more ebullient members of my township, just for the sake of your own good name."

Hopkins transfixed on the Mayor. "I beg your-"

"I do not beg yours!" Randall shouted, "and none of your men's either. Do what you must, Witchfinder, but do so with great haste. I want you out of this town by the week's end or your methods will be reported back to our Parliament in my first correspondence sent to the King. Good night!" He stormed to his home and barged the door.

"Your methods are frightening to our people," Thomas said to Hopkins, "and it is causing much distress to our town. Go, do what you must, with God's blessing, but make haste, for your own sake."

The company of men watched as the Reverend followed the Mayor to his homestead. The door closed behind him.

"Snivelling little…"

"No, Master Stearne, he is simply afraid," Hopkins replied calmly, hiding his own frustration.

"I'm sure we could find a way to tie him in to all this," Lucian added.

"Indeed not, Master Lucian. We must concentrate our efforts on young Ellie Harewood for our own sake. That much of what the good Mayor says is true. And we must make haste. I want her by daybreak tomorrow."

Stearne faced his commander. "Then we must go get the boy, then."

The smile retuned to Hopkins once more. "Indeed we must, Master Stearne, indeed we must."

Sabbath

Ellie stood in the darkness awaiting Luna. Peering through the mass of darkened trunks and vegetation, her night senses slowly emerged. She knew something different was happening this night, unlike the training she had taken thus far. Sister Luna had been secretive about the events of the evening, and this was unnerving. Ellie knew that Wagner would be attending and that they were heading somewhere deep within the forest. Doubt emerged in her mind as to whether she truly was safe in the company of these two forest dwellers, one a witch and one a lycanthrope, but knew there could be no turning back.

Sister Luna and Wagner emerged from the darkness side by side. Apprehension crossed her body, knowing full well they were about to begin.

"Ellie," Wagner said as he approached, "now is the time." For a moment Ellie believed her fear was readable. The lycanthrope placed a hand on her shoulder. "Do not be afraid, you stand in fear to no-one."

"This, you must realise," Luna began, "or you will never achieve the potential of that you can reach."

Wagner extended an arm and gestured Ellie to begin walking. The three left the clearing and passed in to the trees. The cold winds cut deeply, penetrating the gaps in Ellie's shawl.

Ellie attempted to direct her thoughts elsewhere. "Where do you dwell, Wagner? I have yet to see the community in which you live."

She thought a smile crossed his face, but wasn't sure in the darkness. "Not far from Luna, Ellie. You will meet my people soon enough."

The trio wandered through the darkness. Fatigue began to take Ellie as she walked along the trails that pushed between trunks and greenery. Sister Luna was leading with the light of a small lantern just ahead. Frost formed upon the little greenery that existed in these winter months, and tree bark began to glow in Luna's light. The cold air was becoming colder the further they travelled. Ellie wrapped her arms around to restrict heat from escaping, remembering the cold attacking her when she stood bound to the tree, and uttered silent thanks that it had not been this night she had been judged.

They emerged in to a circular clearing. Around them the trunks of lifeless trees stood, twisted and decayed in death. Large rocks scattered throughout, each covered in a layer of frost.

Luna stopped. "Wait," she ordered. Ellie and Wagner stopped and watched the hunched, cloaked figure move into the opening.

"What is it?" Ellie whispered as they watched the hag stoop over the ground.

Wagner paused. "You will see." They could hear the old woman mumbling as she gathered debris from the ground. After a moment or so of this strange routine, Sister Luna clapped her hands and a small fire erupted at her feet. The fire roared, clicking and crackling through the silent forest.

Luna turned to Ellie, and beckoned across. "Come here now, child, now is the time." Ellie gave a brief look to Wagner who nodded. Ellie turned to the hag and made her way across the clearing. Luna smiled a twisted smile as Ellie approached and stretched out her long fingers. The flames from behind illuminated only slightly her terrible features, but enough to see a strange new expression upon her mentor, twisted, almost demonic. "Do not be afraid, Ellie, it is time." Ellie extended a hand to the hag. She was not a tall woman but towered above the deformed witch, now looking to her maliciously. "This, my dear, will be your first Sabbath."

Ellie became afraid and attempted to tug back her hand. Luna's grip tightened. "Fret not, child, a Sabbath is not what you would have been led to believe whilst living in the town yonder."

"Then what is it? A summoning of demons? Sins of the flesh? A celebration of evil?"

"No, my dear, no. You are mistaken. That is the perception that the townspeople have. It is untrue. Listen to me dear, listen to me. It is simply a rite of passage as you begin your study in the dark arts."

"Then what does it involve?" Ellie asked, quaking with fear.

"My dear, you must believe that I will not place you in any harm. You must believe this before we continue." Ellie squirmed uneasily and resigned to escape Luna's grip. "Ellie, you must tell me; do you trust in me, as I do you?" Ellie peered into the eyes of her mentor. Although grotesque, she saw there was an element of truth within the expression. "You must trust me, Ellie," Luna added, gently shaking the wrist that she clasped. Ellie's hair tickled as a gust of wind passed by. Noises emerged from the trees. Luna cocked an ear as the forest came alive. "Do you hear them, Ellie? Do you hear them?" Ellie listened as the sound of voices drifted from the darkness, and as the voices came nearer, entering the clearing, they took the form of chants and groans. A great sense of evil hung in the air. They were no longer alone.

"He is close now!" Luna snapped. She beamed from ear to ear, looking excited as the voices grew louder. "He's here! He's here! You must begin now."

Ellie snapped her hands free. Her heart pounded as fear gripped her body. "Who? What is going on?"

The ground rumbled beneath them. Branches shook and swayed as the quake grew stronger. Wind bellowed through the forest, kicking debris in to the air. Ellie's hair danced erratically in its gusts. Luna's cloak ruffled and buffeted, her hood blown to expose long, thinning hair. Chanting grew louder. Fire exploded in to the sky sending Ellie toppling back. It roared as huge arm emerged from the base. The arm thudded a palm into the ground and pushed downward. Ellie watched fearfully as a head emerged.

"He is here!" Luna shouted again. A face emerged from the flames. Eyes glared brilliant white. A creature roared as another arm drew from the flames and pushed up out of the fire. From the sides of its forehead huge, dark, horns twisted and contorted upwards. The creature stood in the fire, towering some nine feet in height. The beast threw its head backward and roared in to the sky, shaking everything inside the forest. Birds flocked from their nests. Ellie watched on, so scared of the creature she could not move.

"Are you he? Are you the dark Lord whom we serve?" Luna shouted over Hell's flames.

The beast peered down to Luna, speaking in a deep tone. "I am not the one you seek, old hag, but the one summoned on his behalf. Why have you called upon me to leave my realm? For what reason have you contacted me to walk upon this existence?"

"To gain the blessing of our Lord and to inform him of the discovery of one whom I believe has power to eclipse any who have walked before her."

"And where is this person of whom you speak?" it asked, leaning down toward inspect the hag. Ellie felt as though her heart may stop. She trembled at the creature conversing with Luna. The beast's voice was powerful, unlike any ever heard on the Earth before.

Luna turned to Ellie and held out a finger. "She is the one of whom I speak." The creature's gaze followed her direction until meeting the eyes of Ellie. Tears trickled from her eyes.

"So, you are the one?"

Ellie could do nothing more than stare at the creature.

"Answer him!" Luna shouted. A small flash of electricity exploded from her fingertips, jolting Ellie and causing her to yelp out. "Answer him!" she screamed again.

Ellie nodded. "Yes, yes…"

The creature turned back to Luna. "I sense a great power within her, but a struggle to master that which she possesses."

"As do I, but please, give her your blessing, her power will be limitless if we can unlock her mind."

"She is nothing more than a frightened girl!" the creature screeched. "Why should I praise her and inform my master of her intentions when she is so fearful she can hardly stand?"

"But she will grow stronger!"

"She may grow stronger, but she cowers like an insignificant insect about to be crushed. She is an embarrassment to our practice and will not be treated as an equal until she can prove her worth. Be gone! Do not call upon me again until she is ready!" The creature turned to Ellie. Ellie screamed. Dizziness overcame her and she slumped to the ground. The creature laughed heartily and retreated back inside the flames. Wagner ran Ellie. She grasped him tight and sobbed into the furs he bore.

The creature continued to laugh until nothing was left but the fire in which it had returned. The flames flickered and died, leaving the three of them alone once more. Wagner comforted the young woman sobbing in his arms. "Remember one thing, Ellie. What doesn't kill you makes you stronger."

And although troubled, tearful and frightened, Ellie would indeed remember.

Jack

"Get off me!" Jack shouted as Lucian dragged him unceremoniously across the frozen terrain. Hopkins had returned to the site of Ellie's attempted execution, to the tree upon which she had been bound. He followed closely behind the boy, his cape flowing in the breeze that crossed the forest clearing. Stearne, Wade and Thomas settled at the edge of the trees, tending their horses and clutching lanterns that swayed in the wind.

"Do you remember this?" Lucian asked as he dragged the youngster by his simple tunic.

"Of course! What is this, your idea of a joke?"

"Not a joke, boy, but a charge," Hopkins replied as the boy continued to struggle.

"A charge? For what?"

Hopkins heard the fear in Jack's voice and felt pride. He gripped the boy's cheeks with a gloved hand and yanked his head upwards so their eyes met. "For assisting a witch in her escape."

Jack began to struggle. He wriggled and swayed in Lucian's grip. "I did nothing of the sort!"

"Do not test my patience!" Hopkins shot back, releasing his grip, thrusting the boy's head backwards. "A trail leads back to the town and to your lodgings, to your *very* door. Now, the question is, how did the accused manage to escape from this tree, having been bound so professionally by my men?"

"Perhaps they were shoddy in their craftsmanship," Jack replied, still struggling against Lucian's grasp.

Hopkins nodded to Lucian. Lucian released the boy and kicked him away. The force of the attack thrust the young man face first to the ground, jarring his head against the frozen surface.

"For assisting the escape of an accused, you are sentenced to immediate death," Hopkins recited.

Jack turned to face his judges, his nose now bleeding. "What? But I didn't do…"

Lucian lunged and smashed a knee down on Jack's spine. He screamed.

Ellie lurched from sleep and rolled to the floor beside her. She cried out and spun round.

Lucian stood, grabbed Jack by the hair and yanked him to his knees. "Please," Jack sobbed, reduced now to nothing more than a frightened toddler, "I haven't done anything." Hopkins flashed a glance across to Wade and Williams, both ordered to deal with any enquiring eyes that might appear in the darkness. Lucian reached down to his captive and took hold of the fringe. He pulled Jack's hair and exposed his throat, placing the sharp edge of his rapier against the skin. The sharp blade drew a drop of blooded where it rested.

"Ready," said Lucian.

Hopkins drew a deep breath, cupped his hands around his mouth and shouted. "Ellie Harewood, hear me now!"

Ellie's mind filled with the clear voice of Matthew Hopkins from across the forest. "Ellie? What is it?" Luna asked, hobbling quickly across to her.

"I can hear him!" she said. "I can hear the Witchfinder!"

"Settle, my dear, settle! This is the effect of your Familiars! They are showing this to you! Settle!" Sister Luna placed her hands on Ellie's shoulders and rubbed them gently.

"I can't see anything," Ellie told her, "I can just hear his voice."

"You must wait for them to make the full connection. Just be calm, Ellie, this is natural. This is your first experience with your Familiars. You must relax and let them take control." Ellie hesitated before nodding. "Now, close your eyes and let them connect to you. Tell me what you see and hear."

Ellie closed her eyes. She saw nothing but darkness and heard nothing but the sound of branches and twigs rustling in a gentle breeze.

"Ellie Harewood! Your lover stands accused of assisting your escape in to the wilderness, and will meet the punishment of death!"

"No!" Ellie shouted.

"What is it?" Luna asked. Ellie relayed the message. "Ignore him, they're baiting you."

"Ellie Harewood, this is your first and last chance to spare this boy. Deliver yourself to the care of my company and he will be released unharmed," Hopkins ordered. Leaves rattled and whispered as the winds passed between them.

"She's not coming," Lucian said above the wind, the gusts becoming harsher now that they had challenged the witch.

Long dark grass distorted Ellie's vision. The blades parted, allowing her a clear view into the clearing. The shadows cast by trunks and branches hid her fox from the hunters. She looked upon Jack as he knelt on the ground, his head pulled tightly back with the rapier resting against his throat. Lucian hunched over the terrified man, his hat and scarf hiding his face from the foxes view. Hopkins stood beside them looking out into the circle of dense trees that surrounded the clearing.

Hopkins turned to Lucian, his face contorted in anger. "You may begin," he said quietly.

Jack cried out as the rapier moved from his throat. The blade moved up to his lips. With one quick slice the blade cut into Jack's cheek from nose to ear. Jack squealed as blood flooded from the gash.

"No!" Ellie's emotions overcame her judgement and she tried to stand.

Luna pushed down hard, returning Ellie to her seated position. "Sit down!" the hag shouted, jolting Ellie back to consciousness.

Ellie glared at her. "Luna, they're cutting him!"

"Then let them do it!"

"I can't do that!" Ellie replied angrily, "they will kill him!"

"If that is what they intend then that is what must happen!"

Ellie's face became awash with tears. "Let them do it?"

"Where was he, Ellie? Where was this young man of yours when you were trialled for witchcraft?" Ellie looked toward the hag, unable to comprehend her malice. "Answer me! Where was he?"

"He was ... he was..."

"There, Ellie, remember?" Ellie remembered. She saw the townsfolk coming into the clearing where she was bound. "And what did he do to help you?" Luna's voice drifted through the hallucination. Ellie looked towards Jack. Her heart fell.

"Witch," was all she could hear him saying. "Witch!"

"Ellie, help me!" Jack sobbed. "Please, help me!"

"He left you for dead, Ellie. He accused you of witchcraft and left you to die." Ellie remembered his accusation, made in order to save his own life.

"I think we'll have to go further," Hopkins began, unhappy with the silence that had answered his threats. "Tie him to the tree."

Lucian yanked Jack to his feet. The youngster put up little fight. Hopkins held him against the trunk while Lucian tried to bind his hands together , but it quickly became obvious that the tree was too broad for Jack's hands to be tied behind. Lucian tied one end of a sturdy rope to his left hand. Jack yelped as the rope knotted. The hunter then attached the rope to Jack's right hand in the same way, ensuring it was tight against the tree, and Jack was unable to escape.

"Ellie, please," Jack whispered, rolling his head.

"Yes, listen to the boy, Ellie! Appear now, before us, and we will spare his life!" Hopkins shouted in to the forest.

Lucian took hold of the boy's clothing and with one powerful movement tore downward, shredding the shirt and exposing his chest and abdomen. Lucian clasped his rapier. "Ellie Harewood, I implore you to show yourself and accept your punishment immediately!"

Ellie seethed. Gritting her teeth, she watched through her Familiar's eyes. All about them the simple lodge began to tremble. Utensils rattled. The ground swayed. Sister Luna looked around. The door rattled on its latch. The cauldron shook inside the fire pit. A wind gusted around them both.

"Ellie! Help!" Jack croaked. "Please!"

Ellie's eyes, though closed, turned red. She watched as Lucian grazed Jack's abdomen with his blade.

"Last chance, Ellie! Show yourself!" She clearly heard Hopkins' voice. The cauldron tipped from its resting place and rolled on to the floor, flooding its contents through the building. Warm water splashed across the witches, who showed no notice as it sprayed about them. The eaves holding the roof of Luna's home trembled, raining dust and debris down.

Lucian clasped the handle of the rapier with two hands, placing one at the base. Slowly he raised the blade and adopted a stance ready to attack his captive.

Jack turned to see the tip of the blade pointing in his direction. "Ellie!" he screamed.

Hopkins shook his head in frustration, his patience worn thin by the failure of the witch to answer his call. "Do it," he ordered his hunter.

Lucian snarled and charged at Jack.

"Ellie!"

The blade ploughed deep into Jack's abdomen. His screams echoed throughout the forest, ghastly and terrifying.

"No!" Ellie cried. She exploded in to an aura of white light. The door blasted from its hinges. Luna crashed in to the wall.

Jack lurched and squirmed as Lucian withdrew his blade. He gasped, his head limited to small movements.

"Our Father, who art in Heaven," William's voice began from the treeline to the clearing.

"Hush your mouth!" Hopkins snarled. "Do not offer the good Lord's prayers to this heathen!"

The light subsided in Luna's dwelling. Ellie opened her tearful eyes and looked at the carnage. She saw the hag pushing herself upright and rushed across to assist. "I am so sorry," she began, still crying.

"You will learn in time that these hunters will push you to the very limits, emotionally and physically. They baited you as they knew you could not resist the young man."

"I didn't help him," Ellie whispered between her tears. "I could have helped him, and I didn't."

"Such is the change to your conscience, my dear. Remember, he failed to help you when you needed it. No matter whether they love you or hate you, you must think only of yourself, and never anyone else."

As Luna rose to her feet Ellie noticed something strange. The compassion and feelings she had felt towards Jack now subsided. No longer did she feel upset for him, or indeed any responsibility for his murder. She was numb to the pain and carefree. Luna noticed this also. Hopkins had inadvertently triggered the hatred Ellie needed to realise her power. Now she lost empathy for people and remorse for every act she committed, her conscience would no longer restrict her powers or her ability to use it. She was changing.

***

"What now?" Stearne asked Hopkins as he and Lucian returned to their horses.

"Our task has become difficult, that I accept, but we still have an option. Do you remember why we were first summoned here?"

"The hag."

Hopkins watched Stearne's breath plume in the amber light of the lantern. "Exactly. Let's piece together what we know. She haunts these woods and has an effect over the town of Elkwood, so much so that the townspeople have trialled various women themselves for being associated with her."

"It would appear that the hag has a grip over the impressionable, vulnerable women inside the town, does it not?" Lucian asked, apparently unaffected by his recent act of atrocity.

"So, if we neutralise the hag, our young sorceress will be rendered vulnerable," Wade suggested.

"Exactly, Master Wade, exactly." Hopkins grinned. "If you cut the tail from an angry dog, the dog will turn and bite you. But, should you cut the head from the dog's body, the tail is rendered useless and will die of its own accord." Hopkins pulled himself into the saddle. "It is simple, gentlemen. We find the head within this damned forest and sever it."

To Realise

Ellie sat in the crisp winter morning. There was little warmth in the sun that shone through the forest. She had sat on this trunk during the conversation with Sister Luna and Wagner a few nights before. A chilly breeze caressed her neck. Deep in thought, her eyes closed, she reflected.

Something had clicked inside Ellie during Hopkins' attack on Jack last night. She quickly developed a cold, callous frame of mind. This is what Sister Luna encouraged. Witches were hated throughout the country, and, rightly or not, were blamed for many of the wrongdoings or problems that arose within its townships. For a witch to truly thrive she needed to separate herself from the life she once knew and accept the fact that she would be held responsible for tragic events, no matter whom they affected. A witch could have no friends from her former life; many would turn their backs and become accusers, simply to save their own skins. The only acquaintances a witch should have were other witches and people living a paranormal existence, those different to the everyday people existing in a community such as Elkwood. The shock and horror that Ellie experienced through her Familiars last night had proved this was the case, and that henceforth she would be forever alone. When slumped under the furs in an attempt to sleep, she often recalled the situations she had experienced. Sister Luna was right. The two people for whom she cared the most in her previous life, her father and Jack, had accused her of witchcraft and watched her trialled by the Witchfinder, Matthew Hopkins. They had not tried to help. They wanted nothing to do with her. Ellie's sadness turned to anger, then hatred. No longer was there compassion for Jack, nor for her father. Hatred welled with every passing moment. She was no longer the woman she had been.

Luna emerged from her home and watched the trees begin to sway. She looked to the sky. A birch tree creaked, as though being twisted and contorted by a giant, unforeseen force. The branches splintered as the force took hold, each point moving towards Ellie. A whirlwind of leaves and forest debris swirled within the air and fluttered across the opening. The gusts reached Sister Luna, who placed a hand atop her hood to keep it from flapping off. Magically, stones uprooted from the earth, dropping soil as they emerged from the terrain. Luna looked on in amazement. The stones swirled in a circular motion above Ellie. Trees moaned. The whirlwind of fallen leaves and twigs circled upwards into the sky. Ellie's hair flapped wildly in the storm, though the winds had little sound other than a whistle.

"I can do anything," Luna heard Ellie whisper, who slowly opened her eyes. Ellie looked to the trees with a menacing gaze. "I can do anything," she repeated once more. Slowly, Luna began to levitate from the forest floor. She gasped in surprise and grabbed at the doorframe.

"Ellie," Luna said, calmly. "Ellie!"

"I understand now," Ellie replied, "the only restrictions to my power are the ones I create for myself."

"Correct, Ellie, now please!"

Ellie turned and saw Luna levitating from the doorway. Everything fell. Stones thudded to the ground. Trees returned to their natural positions. The leaves rustled as they fluttered to the earth, no longer caught in a breeze, and Luna fell to the floor with a bump. "I am so sorry!" Ellie shouted, leaping up from her position. She jumped the log and ran to the fallen hag.

Luna cackled quietly away to herself as Ellie approached. "Well done, my dear, well done. You're now realising your own potential."

Ellie crouched beside her mentor. "Are you all right?"

Luna looked to her and smiled. "Never better."

Plan

"Master Randall, we will require its full use, no questions asked I am afraid," Hopkins bellowed through the empty barn. It was littered with hay and stalls and occupied by two horses. It was dark, but dry and comfortable.

"I say you, this is becoming quite ridiculous," Mayor Randall replied, placing a palm across his forehead. "What more do you want from us?"

Hopkins grinned. "Nothing more, my good man, nothing more. This is where we intend to keep her as there is nowhere else available to us."

"So, you found where she is hiding?" Randall asked, removing the hand from his head and placing it upon his hip.

Hopkins wandered over to the dignitary and placed his hands on the Mayor's shoulders. "My friend, we are near. We must make preparations to detain her, and in doing so we will deliver to you the hag whom is roaming these cursed trees."

"That is all well and good, Master Hopkins, but pray tell how you manage to restrain young Ellie Harewood if she is as strong as you believe?"

Hopkins kept his smile and fumbled in his pocket. Brushing aside his cape, he held out his gloved hands. Between his thumb and fingers rested two tacks.

"Tacks!" Randall gasped. "How on Earth will they restrain a witch of such power?"

"On this you must trust me, my good man. Simply allow us the use of this sturdy barn to keep her restrained, and I swear that the hag will be delivered to you, to trial as you see fit."

Randall wandered through the barn. "All right." He turned to Hopkins and pointed a finger. "This is your last chance, Witchfinder. You deliver on this, you must promise, or notice of your exploits will be sent to London by letter and your services will no longer be required."

"I make you now that promise, Master Randall, and will keep it in my heart. Of that you have my word."

The Mayor brushed past the Witchfinder and opened the barn door. He was greeted by the townsfolk who had congregated outside, all having heard different versions of the events that had taken the Mayor there. "Collect the fire wood! We will have a witch to burn!" he shouted.

Wolves

Ellie and Luna entered a small clearing along a lonely forest trail. The sun fell as they made their way to attend Wagner and his people. Ellie was excited but also a little apprehensive. She had wanted to see the community in which he lived, but the fear of the last lycanthrope attack she witnessed whilst still a member of the Elkwood community remained fresh within her mind. She walked beside Luna, who walked with large, wooden staff to assist her on this journey. Ellie wore the old shawl given her by Luna; she wore it consistently as it protected her from the biting winds.

The clearing opened at a cross roads where many different trails merged into one. Luna turned to her. "Just a moment, my dear."

"What is it, Luna? Is everything all right?" Ellie asked. She was still concerned about the fall Luna had experienced, the fall which had been her own doing.

Luna smiled. "Of course, Ellie, I am fine. Come here, I want to show you something. This is the reason I stumble." Luna held out an arm and gestured for Ellie to pass. Ellie did so, and looked at the crossroads in the dwindling light.

"What is it I'm looking for?" Ellie asked, her eyes darting back and forth between the trees.

"Wait but a moment, my dear. You will see." They stood there for a moment, Ellie frowning as she looked within the trees.

A hint of excitement tainted Luna's voice. "Did you see?"

"I did," Ellie replied, unknowing what it was she had witnessed. A bright, red light had emerged from the darkness for a second and vanished as mysteriously as it appeared. A green light shone, and disappeared. Then blue. Then yellow. They were engulfed by hundreds of coloured lights, each one dancing around them. Some vanished, some remained. Some flickered, some twinkled, but all swarmed silently within the darkness, illuminating the two women in

121

a plethora of different colours. "Luna, what are they?" Ellie asked, astonished at the phenomenon. She turned to the hag, who bore a peaceful smile upon her face.

"They are the most elusive of phenomena that exist within our world," Luna began, holding a finger out into the darkness. "They can only be witnessed by beings born or brought in to our world."

"Our world?"

"The world of witches, lycanthropes, vampires and the like. No normal human being will ever bear witness to the beauty which is on show for us now." A shimmering, mauve light perched itself on the end of Luna's outstretched finger. Luna presented it to Ellie. "Take a look, see," she told her, raising her hand to Ellie's eyes. Ellie peered into the fantastic light, squinting against its brightness. Inside it stood a small, female form. Her clothing had been tailored from flower petals, leaves and grass. She glowed with a light created by two butterfly-like wings fluttering from her back. "Fairies," Luna explained, hypnotised by the creature which she held. "The fact that you can see these amazing beings suggests that you are advancing in your ability, Ellie. You are becoming stronger and will continue to do so each and every day." Ellie continued to look at the beautiful creature and its dazzling light until Luna jolted her finger gently, prompting the fairy back in to the air. "It's a sign, Ellie. Great things lie ahead for you. Now then, make haste."

The two witches moved slowly through the fairy lights, along the trail and towards Wagner's dwellings. The sign was definitely there. Unbeknown to Ellie, she was indeed becoming stronger.

Wagner greeted them both in the darkness. Ellie's night senses emerged as they made their way through the forest. The air clamped down on them with sharp teeth as the winter's night set in across the land. Wagner placed a hand on her shoulder, and smiling, he gestured with the other towards a fire that burned in the darkness.

Ellie followed Luna between two simple structures, huts of some kind, similar to the one she now shared with her mentor, made of forest materials. Around the fire sat people of all ages. Ellie shocked at their large number. They wore tattered and torn clothing made from furs of animals such as deer and fox. Sympathy and sadness for these people engulfed her. Even though they smiled and greeted with apparent joy, it was clear that they were suffering. Their dirty faces, poor hygiene and exposure to the elements were clear to see. They did not have the luxury of a home like the one she had lived in back in Elkwood.

Ellie returned the people's gaze with a brief, nervous smile. She joined Luna and sat beside the fire, defying of the night's bitter coldness.

"These, Ellie, are my people," Wagner explained. "They are good people, like you. And like you, they have been spurned by society. "

"It is a sad state that we find ourselves in, in this day and age," Luna replied, patting Wagner's knee as he sat beside her.

Wagner smiled and placed his arm around Agnieszka who had joined them.

"Hello Ellie," came a small voice from by the fire. Ellie turned to a young boy, no older than five years, wave across to her. Ellie smiled and waved back. He was sitting beside a woman whom Ellie believed to be his mother.

"Hello, and what is your name?" she asked jovially. Feeling her expression change, Ellie remembered the last time she smiled with joy. It had been back in Elkwood, walking from the church to the town in Jack's company.

"My name is Azur," the boy replied.

"And a fine name it is, too," Sister Luna told him, smiling her grotesque, but in this instance, pleasant smile. Sister Luna truly was a grotesque, haggard old woman, and Ellie wondered if the young boy may have been frightened by her earlier in his life.

"Now, Ellie, these are my people," Wagner explained, gesturing to those surrounding the fire. "We are a simple, peaceful tribe, but we have been spurned by the township from whence you came."

"Elkwood?" Ellie asked, momentarily confused.

"Yes, Elkwood." He looked to the fire. "The town spurned us, damned us to live in this existence which you see around you. When they learned of our curse they banished us here to the wilderness, to the farthest reaches of this forest." Ellie knew they were lycanthropes and realised now it was this particular pack that had terrorised Elkwood when she lived there. Wagner smiled once more as he looked to Luna. "But now, Sister Luna is helping us to master that curse."

The hag turned to the Ellie. "And I will need you to continue my work."

"But how? What can I do to help these people?"

"Ellie, I have brought you here tonight so that the lycanthropes may help you in your quest," she replied.

"We know of your debt, and we will help," said Agnieszka.

"Samael is a very devious person, Ellie. If you bargain with him you must honour your debt, or face the cost with your very life," Wagner explained. He poked at the fire with a broken tree branch.

"And with mine," Luna reminded her pupil. "Ellie, these good people can assist you if we can unlock their powers. They will aid you and protect you during your quest, but we must overpower the curse so that they may use it to their advantage."

"It is not a curse," Agnieszka snapped. Ellie detected a hint of frustration in the young woman. "We are only a handful of creatures, but we exist throughout the continent. This is a natural occurrence and one to which we were born. This is our evolution. Just as man evolves into different races and creeds, we are but a part of that evolution."

"And we are almost there, Ellie. I know what I need to do for these people, but, alas, my power is not strong enough for me to do so." Luna looked to her hands.

"But if you're not strong enough how can we assist?" Ellie questioned them all.

"My dear, I am not the strongest witch in attendance this night." Ellie looked from Luna to Wagner. "Me? You mean me?"

Luna nodded. "Yes, Ellie. You."

"But, I don't know if I can-"

"Of course you can!" Luna snapped, "have you learnt nothing from these past few days? Have you not witnessed the raw powers that harbour within you? Levitation of objects, for example? Connection with your Familiars? The sights you have witnessed? The demon? The fairies?" She pointed back to the forest and toward the trail where the lights had appeared. She then sighed. "You must believe, Ellie. As soon as you do, you will know no limits. Have some belief in yourself."

"The forest is talking of you, Ellie," Wagner added. "It speaks of a great witch of power, unequalled by any living creature that walks across the Earth."

"The forest talks?"

"It does," Agnieszka replied. "If you listen closely enough, it will speak. It is alive."

Ellie looked around the fire to the people who placed so much in her inexperienced hands. She felt like a witch, from the destruction and chaos already created by her own hand, but did not feel as powerful as Sister Luna believed.

"Ellie, I believe you are very strong," Azur said from across the fire. She looked to him and smiled. The young boy smiled back.

"I will help you through this. Follow my lead and we will see," said Luna.

Ellie looked toward the people once more, at their miserable existence and the poverty to which they were cursed. "What must I do?"

"My dear, first you must understand. Lycanthropes are created from the cursed one's brain. Are you familiar with anatomy?"

"A little."

"Within the brain are many fluids," Wagner began. "In our case, those liquids do not flow the same as a humans. It is known that when the moon is full the tides of the seas affect these, thus affecting our being."

"Really?" Ellie asked, astonished by the very thought. Such beliefs had never been considered amongst the self-sufficient community where she had once lived.

"It is true. The moon has an effect much like a pull. It can sway the tides and affect them dramatically," Agnieszka added in her broken English.

"The moon affects most liquids, even those that exist inside us," Luna continued. "A human can experience emotions such as rage or anger, and can become completely unpredictable when the moon is full. For these people, the liquids within their brains act erratically, reducing the organ to a primitive state. The brain believes it is a different creature, a wolf, and sends signals to the body to become such. That's when the change begins. That is when the human becomes the wolf, and the effect lasts as long as the full moon hangs in the night skies. When it vanishes, so does the animal. All we must do, Ellie, is use our power to simulate the effect of a full moon and the animal will emerge."

Wagner nodded. "If you can do this for us, Ellie, we can help protect you from the townspeople, and from your witch hunter."

"Your Familiars sent you a warning, my dear. He is hunting you for certain. You escaped his wrath, and for that he will be relentless in his pursuit. He is experienced in dealing with beings like us, and I do not believe I can protect you without Wagner's help. You must be protected, Ellie. You are in an extremely vulnerable position. I have limited power, and nothing near strong enough to protect either of us should he come calling. Soon you will be strong and able to repel the King's entire armies if you should wish to do so, but an army of wolves that will answer to your call can be most useful."

"If you can grant us this one desire and control our change to animal form, we will protect you until the end. We should not be forced to live in such terrible conditions, and nor should Luna or you be forced from society because of your gifts. We have all been judged by the humans, and for that they will pay with their lives."

A surge of anger gripped Ellie. With both her father and lover denouncing her a witch to the entire community of Elkwood, she knew first-hand the evils of mankind. She would never forgive them for that, not ever. "What must I do?" Ellie asked Luna.

"Imagine a full moon, that is all. Nothing more, nothing less."

"A full moon…"

This time she did not close her eyes. A wave of confidence replaced the anger. A full moon. She saw one in her mind's eye, burning bright against a sheet of pure darkness. The clear grey ridges and mounds on its surface across the vast distance where it resided appeared clearly, even across the vast distance, and the rings that emit from its shine on a clear, starry night could be seen in the cloudless skies.

Wagner twitched. Hair sprouted on his arm.

"It's working!" Luna whispered. Around the campfire Ellie watched the lycanthropes jerk and contort. she gazed into the darkness, focusing upon the moon that she had created. The lycanthropes began to cough. Cracks echoed out as bones contorted and shifted in their bodies. Some rolled to the floor. Agnieszka placed her hands upon some dried leaves as fingers morphed to claws. Screams of bellowed between the trees. Bones broke, muscles tore and bodies contorted. Ellie heard the pain in their cries, could hear the torment in their voices, but remained focused. The quiet, caring girl she had once been was now no more. A tinge of concern existed somewhere in her subconscious, but quickly vanished as she revelled in the power. The people around her broke. Blood spurted from abrasions and injuries, but still she continued. The moon glowed within the depths of her mind. Clouds thundered past, illuminated in its bright light. Wagner's head snapped back. His jaw and nose broke and pushed out. He screamed. Ellie's anger surged. It roared throughout her body. Her mind opened. Below the moon she saw a town burning. The houses fuelled a gigantic fire, one that swept throughout the entire township. People screamed. Muscle and bone exposed as skin melted away in the intense heat. Some quivered on their knees, screaming and crying, the sounds of their terror merging with the wailing of the lycanthropes around the campfire. Then, walking towards her through the carnage, through the blood and death, was the flowing figure of her mother. The apparition moved gracefully, as though through water as her hair and dress rippled around her. Her eyes gleamed white.

The phantom looked to Ellie. "They will fear you." Blood trickled from her hairline and streamed across her face, now one of utter malevolence and purest evil. "They will fear you!"

Ellie's eyes opened. The carnage around the fire had diminished. A howl pierced the winter air. In the clearing, illuminated by the fierce fire, stood the community she had journeyed to meet; only now they were no longer human. Wolves now existed, their breath snorting and misting into the cold air. Brilliant, amber eyes met hers. A large wolf crossed the debris and stood almost eye to eye. The ground quaked with the rumble from inside its chest. It stood shoulder height to the witch with a coat a plethora of different browns. The muzzle was hardly distinguishable, so black was its shade. Ellie looked into the wolf's eyes and recognised something human and familiar. There was intelligence behind them. Any sense of hesitation had now vanished. The belief of power was stronger now, stronger than it had ever been. She sensed the energy waking within. Now content, she held out her right hand towards the wolf's shaggy coat. The wolf held eye contact. The growl increased.

Slowly Ellie placed the hand on the beast's neck and began to pet. "Wagner?" she asked, running fingers through his coat.

"Indeed it is," came Sister Luna's voice. Ellie had all but forgotten about the witch accompanying her.

Looking about the camp Ellie noticed the pack of wolves staring from the darkness, their strange eyes glowing from the reflection of the fire. A small wolf, no bigger than a dog, caught her attention. This had to be Azur.

"These people need you," Luna continued as Ellie stroked the lycanthrope. "They live in fear of your people, your townsfolk, who judge them with fear and prejudice. These are merely creatures attempting to live in peace."

"How can I help them, though? How can I assist them to find peace?"

"You already have, my dear, you already have."

Wagner snorted and turned away from the witches. They both stood and watched as the lycanthropes gathered together before disappeared in to the forest.

"Where are they going?" Ellie asked, the warmth of the fire caressing her body once again.

"They will venture out to test the spell you have cast upon them."

"A spell?" Ellie asked.

"Yes, my dear. That is the first spell you have cast." Luna nodded toward the vanishing wolves. "The sheer power of that which you have used must be praised. Many witches practice for a lifetime and can do nothing more than extinguish a flame." A strange, powerful wind sighed past Ellie and attacked the campfire. "You must look out for these people, Ellie. They are weak when not in their animal form. Governed by the power of the moon, they can only protect themselves fully when the beasts are unleashed. The townspeople know this too, and will hunt them whilst the moon is gone, free from fear." Ellie watched as the last tails vanished into the darkness. "By turning them to wolf when they so request, you can offer more in protection for this clan than they can give themselves. In return they will remain as loyal to you as your Familiars."

"And that is all I need to do? Imagine a moon?" Ellie asked the witch.

"Such is your power, Ellie. You are believing now in your ability, and through this you'll become stronger. Already you are feeling it."

The change that Luna spoke of was now more than just a coincidence. Ellie enjoyed the aggression to which she was succumbing, and the hatred against her father for accusing her. She was changing and knew it. Now there was a feeling of compassion for the witch who had saved her life and to Wagner and his people, seeing just how they lived in fear from the township of Elkwood, the town from where she was raised. The Witchfinder General posed such a great threat to their kind, and something had to be done to protect these people, and of course, herself.

These matters preyed on Ellie's mind as they wandered back towards Luna's lodgings. The experienced witch had called upon the fairies to navigate the way back, illuminating their trail with a host of bright and wondrous colours. Everything made sense. Everything fell into place. Something emerged within thought as they wandered through the forest. The dreams about her mother were intensifying. Her mind was changing and becoming more powerful. She thought that somehow, someway, her mother may have something to do with this. Although the way in which she appeared within the dreams were distressing, Ellie knew of the love that existed between them whenever they met inside the dream world. This thought warmed her heart. This bond to her mother would bind them always, and this, for the first time in her life, made her happy. Her mother was encouraging the strange, new gift, and she would make her proud.

Emotions

Ellie awoke from a pleasant, dreamless sleep. The sunshine beamed through the window in four bright shafts, catching the dust in its golden haze. She pushed up to her elbows and looked for Luna. Listening to the hag potter outside brought a smile to her lips. Never once had Luna slept since she'd arrived.

Wrapping a shawl around, Ellie strolled out in to the sharp, cold morning. The sky was blue; not even a hint of a cloud passed through its vast openness. Sister Luna grinded flowers together between two stones. This had awoken Ellie from her slumber.

Luna turned and smiled. "Good morning."

"Good morning."

Luna dropped the rock she was holding and wiped her hands against her cloak. "Guess who came by here this morning?" she asked, shuffling towards Ellie. Ellie frowned, shaking her head. "It was Wagner, Ellie, and Agnieszka. And you know what?"

"No, what?"

"And...they were still in their wolf form!" Luna gasped excitedly, placing her hands on Ellie's arms. "They were still wolves! Ellie, you did it! Not even the daylight could change them back!"

"They were still in wolf form?" Ellie repeated in disbelief.

"They were! The spell you created has eclipsed even the power I thought you capable of."

For the remainder of the morning the women sat outside drinking herbal brews boiled in the cauldron. Sister Luna explained to her apprentice the many theories about the opening of one's mind. Ellie truly believed whatever it was she could imagine, she would indeed create.

"Have there ever been witches before, like me? Ones who possess the same ability that I am learning?"

Luna pulled a strange face. "Some. There are tales from around the country that speak of witches with power. Very few, though, tell tales of an ability such as yours. Yes, basic spells which frighten townsfolk, but only have I ever known of two stories in which women hold significant powers."

"I'd like to hear about them," Ellie asked politely.

"Well, my dear, there is nothing of much to speak. I am aware of a coven known as the Pendle Witches who practiced in the north – west of the country. They were a devilish lot. Very powerful, and very evil. There were two grand witches, by the names of Chattox and Demdike. The atrocities they created were unthinkable, even for me to consider. Both were finally caught and trialled, although their coven lives long to this day. There was also coven practising in these very trees, when I was but a girl. Three of them; each known only by surnames. Miss Brock, Miss Lake and Miss O'Connor. They haunted these trees during their lives, keeping hidden from view, much like we do now. They were purest of evil, though. Every now and again people would vanish from the town. It mattered not of man, woman or child, someone will disappear, never to return. Most likely, these people were used for rituals and sacrifices. Spilling innocent blood is one way to appease the demons of Hell, but I never considered such a deed. Those three witches still haunt this forest, albeit in spirit form. In fact, it is these three who prey on the innocent travellers upon Elkwood's boundary, and not me as the town believes."

"But we have never encountered them, not yet."

Luna lifted a palm upright. A blue haze appeared around the grounds and dwelling of her home, separating both witches from the forest. "My land is protected, as is the land where the lycanthropes dwell. The spirits are unable to penetrate these barriers."

"Do the spirits pose a threat, even to fellow witches?" Ellie asked.

The blue haze around them disbanded. "My dear, some witches are of the purest evil, and care not for their fellow kin. These three witches, Brock, Lake and O'Connor, are beings of similar intent. Although the forest is vast in which they roam, one day they will stumble upon those living within. It is best to be safe, Ellie. Caution is a valuable attribute. Ghosts can be troublesome at the best of times, but when their soul is crafted with the worst intentions, their threat is to anyone and everyone, regardless."

The pair had returned indoors when Ellie became aware of a situation happening way across the forest.

"Ellie? Ellie what is it?" Luna asked.

Ellie leant forward and prepared for something she knew would happen. An image appeared with her mind. A screaming, inconsolable woman filled her vision. "My Familiars," Ellie replied, "they have made the connection." She swayed gently. "The spell has run its cause," she added, recognising the troubled woman as Azur's mother. "Oh no," she gasped, placing a hand across her mouth.

"What, child? What is the matter?"

Tears began to sting their way forward. "Oh no." Wagner stooped down on the forest floor. His face showed dismay and torment. In his arms was the small body of a blood-soaked child which he drew close to his own, naked body. Agnieszka screamed as she looked at the injured body he held. The three lycanthropes turned and darted between the trees.

"It's Azur," Ellie cried out, "he's been seriously hurt. He's bleeding heavily."

Luna jumped to her feet. "They're bringing him here." Quickly she began grabbing at her jars and herbs. "What else do you see?" she asked tersely as Ellie continued with her Familiars.

Cyrius soared through the air and came to rest upon a high tree branch. "I'm with Cyrius." Luna cleared a space on the floor next to the cauldron. Tears tickled Ellie's cheeks. She looked upon four men tracking through the wilderness. "It's him. It's the Witchfinder."

Luna stopped her clearing momentarily. The Witchfinder.

Ellie embraced the connection to her owl and submerged within the forest. "...to be sure. You must remain cautious. It was a truly blessed shot, Daniel."

"I've never known of or seen a lycanthrope during daylight hours. It appeared to be much smaller than a full grown adult, maybe a juvenile or child. It may have been a dog, but I was not willing to take that chance," Ellie heard the marksman reply. "I'd take the chance to kill a lycanthrope, even if mistaken about its identity. They all deserve to die."

"You are correct, young Master. I am proud of your accomplishment." Ellie grimaced with anger at the sound Hopkins' voice.

"No!" she shouted, gnashing her teeth together.

"Ellie calm!" Luna ordered. Anger surged through Ellie's being. The power led to confidence. Rage intensified with every passing second.

"Ellie!"

Ellie opened her eyes and looked towards Luna. "Do not worry. I am in full control."

"Indeed you are, but you must help me now. They will be bringing him here for help."

With a swift swipe of her arm, an invisible force passed through the room. The image of a wind sweeping through the home had materialised into reality from Ellie's mind. She looked to the cauldron and raised her palm upwards. The cauldron bubbled and spewed water from its brim, hissing as it flooded down on the hot coals and firewood.

Luna threw a tattered carpet across the floor. "I need Comfrey," she said, kneeling down to flatten its creases. She pointed Ellie to the shelf that held many herbs and flowers. Ellie jumped to her feet and rushed across. "Broad leaves and a black root," Luna described as she scanned the shelf.

"It's not here." Luna shot a look of disbelief. Ellie's heart sank. The lycanthropes were rushing through the forest to seek Luna's help and there was little she could do. "Wait," Ellie gasped as a thought struck her, "where can I find it?"

"It can be found in a damp, grassy area such as a river bank or ditch."

Ellie nodded. Closing her eyes she lifted her left palm out towards the sunlight coming through the door, and focused on the darkness engulfing her. "Streak, Cyrius, hear me." She spoke calmly within the confines of her own mind. "You must find me the plant which we so desperately need. It bares large, broad leaves and has a black root. It is known to humans as Comfrey, but to you it may be known by a different name. Please find this herb and return it to me at once. The life of a child depends on it." The vast forest drifted beneath her. Cyrius had taken control. "By a river bank or inside a ditch." Now, she bounded across the terrain, brushing through grass and shrubbery as she rode with Streak.

"Luna!" Wagner's voice emerged from outside.

"Wagner! In here!" she replied frantically. Agnieszka and Wagner burst in through the open door, followed quickly by Azur's mother. "Lay him down," she ordered. Wagner stooped down and carefully placed the fragile body of the child on the blanket. Quickly he stood and stepped back allowing Luna to begin work. Ellie handed them the furs she slept under as she made her way over. They took them without acknowledgement, their focus clearly for the injured child that lay before them.

"Please, please," Azur's mother whispered between the tears. Wagner comforted her.

Luna closed her eyes and held out her hands above the unconscious child. "I call forth now the Goddess of the Night, to hear our plea for a fading life, and help us heal this child with strength and might. I call forth now the Goddess of the Night, to hear our plea for a fading life, and help us heal this child with strength and might."

Ellie recoiled back to her Familiars. Cyrius had found the Comfrey on small river bank just as Luna had stated. He hooted out through the daylight. Streak clearly heard his call. Both he and Ellie looked up to see the owl perched on a branch overhanging the herb. They saw the darkened green leaves of the Comfrey. Streak clawed at its root.

Luna circled her hands above Azur and looked down upon his injury. A deep puncture wound opened his lower abdomen, on the right-hand side below the ribs. A silver arrow embedded in his body and already the effect of the silver was showing. Blood clotted and a scab was forming, but it was still bleeding. It trembled. Agnieszka sobbed. The arrow quivered and began to push from the wounded flesh. It shook as it emerged and popped from his body, thudding gently beside him. With the arrow came more fresh blood which splattered onto the blanket and across the floor.

Ellie raised a palm and levitated the arrow to eye level. It floated closer so she could determine from which element it had been forged. Sister Luna and the lycanthropes looked on as the young woman exercised her power and drew the arrow closer.

"It's silver," Wagner sighed.

"May the Goddess protect him," Luna whispered, returning her gaze to the injured child.

"What's wrong?" Ellie asked as she released her power and dropped the arrow.

"Silver is our bane, and the bane of many others," Agnieszka began, wiping the tears from her eyes. "We suffer from a reaction to it, like an allergy, and should we come in to contact with silver that is pure, we die."

Azur's mother continued to sob. Ellie journeyed with Streak as he headed back to her, clasping the Comfrey between his jaws.

"My Familiars are coming, they have the herb."

"Then there may still be time. Quickly!" Luna gestured for Ellie to kneel beside her. Ellie slumped down heavily. "If the Witchfinder's men were the ones who attacked Azur they would certainly have used the purest of silver. Azur is in mortal danger. You must help him. You are the only one of us strong enough to do so." Ellie glanced toward her mentor. "Halt the injury. Stop his infection." Ellie nodded. She could do it. She knew it. The belief in her own ability was so great she knew she could help. The feeling of confidence and superiority flowed. "Do whatever you feel necessary."

"I will." Ellie closed her eyes and uttered no spell. She knew no spell, instead channelling the power. Inside her mind appeared Azur, laying on the blood-stained blanket. She lifted her hands. Black liquid ooze from his wound, the result of the infection the silver had caused. The darkened veins within his body became clean. Ellie watched his body glow. She waved her hands above the child and moved them toward the injury. Infection poured from him.

"They are here," Luna whispered softly.

Ellie opened her eyes. "Streak, drop the Comfrey please?" she asked the fox as he cantered inside the home. He complied with his mistress and put the herb down beside her. Cyrius swooped in through the entrance and came to rest on the beams above. "Cyrius, please?" Cyrius beat his wings. The breeze pulsed around the dwelling. With her left hand she gestured upwards, lifting the Comfrey from the ground and into the air. She passed her left hand across her body, mirroring the herb's motion as it floated across the room. The plant swirled within the vortex Cyrius created and separated into many pieces. The leaves shredded and roots separated. A mini tornado of debris and shredded herb swirled above them. Ellie summoned the water boiling inside the cauldron to snake upwards into the air. A small mass of water separated from the rest and rose until it merged with the tornado. The water joined the herb and both flowed within the vortex. It mixed and merged until the concoction was complete, before slithering down towards the child. Cyrius gave one final beat of his wings and rested, allowing Ellie to assume control. The water fell from the air, as if contained in a thin tube and settled on the wound, before smothering the injury and sealing it. Azur coughed. Ellie looked down on him with sadness. The child groaned and sighed. Beads of sweat had formed on his forehead as the silver reacted inside his body.

"There is nothing more you can do," Luna whispered. Ellie watched as the woman took a rag and gently patted the sweat away from the child's skin. All fell silent. The laboured breathing of the child had stopped.

Agnieszka frowned, pursing her lips together. "Azur?"

The child released a single gasp, then nothing more.

"Azur!" his mother screamed. She fell beside his head and bowed over him. "No!" Her grief spread throughout the others. "No!" she screamed before nestling in to his neck, sobbing as she did. "Oh no!"

Wagner sat back on the floor, one hand holding him upright, the other rubbing his forehead. Tears trickled from Agnieszka's eyes. The child was gone.

The sting of emotion attacked Ellie once again, noticing the boy had taken hold of her hand during his last moments. She trembled before releasing it. Agnieszka and Luna huddled around Azur's mother, attempting to offer comfort. The sorrow within the home hung heavy, like a large pendant burdened to a frail body.

Ellie left the lycanthropes to grieve their loss and entered the forest. Cyrius and Streak both followed their mistress to their own habitat. Streak weaved around her legs as she wandered slowly in to the clearing, looking up to her. She stooped down and patted him. "Go on, now, the pair of you. Thank you so much for your efforts." The Familiars gave one last look at their mistress and dashed in to the trees. Streak vanished into the undergrowth and shrubs, and Cyrius swooped high into the sky. Alone with her thoughts Ellie sat down on a rock and sighed. The light passing of a teardrop ran along her cheek.

She had been useless. The lycanthropes had gone to the witches for assistance to save the boy's life and she could not do it. She had been powerless to stop Samael from taking him. Even though her powers had increased and her belief grown stronger, she had been useless to help Azur.

"There was nothing more you could do," came a voice, jolting her from thought. Sister Luna shuffled her awkward frame through the clearing.

"Then why do I feel that there was?" she replied tersely.

Luna perched herself next to Ellie. "Ellie, whether you are a child of the dark arts or not, there will always be a time when you call yourself into question and have doubts about your being. This is a lesson of life, and life affects us all, from a person who dwells within the township of Elkwood, to the smallest insect scurrying the undergrowth inside this forest. What distinguishes each and every one of us, though, is what we learn from life as time passes." She placed a bony hand on Ellie's knee. "No matter how strong you are or how much you have advanced in your powers, no one can resurrect the dead, not one of us. There are only a number of beings capable of such acts, one company being the Lord above and his angels, the other our lord in Hell and his minions. In truth, Azur died when the arrow entered his body. No one could have saved him."

"But he was there, breathing right in front of me!" Ellie cried, her tears flowing as she succumbed to emotion. "I did everything I could and it was not enough!"

"You did everything, you are right, but there is nothing more now that you can do. You must remember this feeling, Ellie. This emotion. This rage. This is what you must draw from all of this. When you stand against those that did this, remember Azur, and you do it for him. You do it for the lycanthropes who have lived in fear for centuries and have been forced to live outside society. Take nothing more with you except the rage and anger which you feel."

Ellie's emotion subsided. Deep down the anger of which Luna had spoken became more contained. Instead of releasing it, for now at least, it would be subdued until needed. To release her frustration and anger at this point would cause destruction to her surroundings, but for the first time she consciously wanted those responsible to feel her power and wrath.

The lycanthropes emerged from Luna's home. Wagner held Azur in his arms, wrapped in furs. "Will you come with us?" he asked quietly. "We will return him to the Earth." Ellie's eyes flooded. She nodded, unable to communicate in any other way.

"Of course," Luna replied.

***

Lucian wandered through the forest. The overcast skies gave it sense of foreboding. The space between the trees seemed darker than usual. Birds called in the hidden depths of the wood. Reverend Jones followed closely behind, still clutching tightly at his crucifix. Lucian knew the Reverend was nervous. He heard the tell-tale signs of the cautious footfalls. "How far?" the Reverend asked as they moved through the vegetation.

"Not far," Lucian whispered from beneath his scarf. His eyes darted back and forth as he took notice of each and every detail. "I can feel their presence."

He brushed between outstretched branches until he stumbled into a small clearing. Underneath his hat the scarf lifted as he smiled. "Is this it?" Jones asked from behind.

Lucian nodded. "It is."

Time

Azur returned to the Earth. The community to which the young boy belonged attended to show their respect. Many in attendance grieved, but not Ellie. Her grief was in the past, now. As she watched the cloth-bound body being covered with earth, only anger existed. Her time was near. Initially she had been afraid of the power, and also of the deal which Luna had made with Samael, but now welcomed her fate with open arms. The evil within consumed any part of the Ellie Harewood who once existed. She wanted to kill. She wanted to seek vengeance on those who had not only wronged her but wronged this community, robbing an innocent little boy of his life. The anxiety turned to excitement. She was ready.

The lycanthropes withdrew to carry out a secret ritual away from the rest of the world. The witches left, allowing the service to continue away from outsider eyes.

The day drew onward. Grey skies merged with darker clouds appearing ominously on the horizon, hinting at the approach of a storm. Ellie sensed that the afternoon, although cold, was not as sharp as it had been previously, and hoped that this was a sign of the changing seasons.

"He went to the right place," a voice drifted from between the trees. Ellie and Luna turned to see the form of a man approaching them.

"He was not used to barter with?" Luna asked as he made his way across.

Samael emerged from the darkness. He bore a sympathetic smile and shook his head. "No, not at all. I took him straight to the light. You have my word that he is safe."

Ellie scowled toward him. "Safe or not, he will be avenged."

Samael smiled, this time benevolently. "And mark my words, young woman; those who wronged him will suffer in the afterlife. I promise."

Ellie turned to Luna. "I want a Sabbath," she said aggressively. A look of concern crossed the hag's face. "Ellie, are you…"

"Luna, I am ready. I can feel it. I want to be the power of which you speak. I feel different, I feel alive. Everything you told me from the start I now believe. I know I am ready."

"You realise that should we call the servant of the Dark Lord it will claim you, if you are not yet powerful enough to stand against it. You must be certain you are ready. I cannot protect you if this should happen."

In the growing darkness a strange light emerged. Ellie looked at Luna and Samael with burning, red eyes. Luna, who had never feared anything in the natural world, took a step backward. "I am ready," came the young woman's reply. "Nothing will stop me now, not after the hurt and grief that has been bestowed by man throughout this forest. Call to the demon."

The fire bathed the trees as its light flickered across their rugged trunks. The dry bracken popped as it fuelled the flames. Ellie recalled her unease the last time they summoned the dark minion. She remembered the fear surging throughout her, and the terror that seized when the servant of the Dark Lord appeared in his master's place. She had been so naïve then. It now felt a lifetime ago, but during a lifetime people change and learn from their experiences. Ellie stood before the fire knowing what to expect and confident she could stand the judgement of whatever Hell-spawn should emerge.

The fire roared, expelling a heat so powerful it may have been drawn from the very depths of the realm she intended to contact.

"It is ready," Sister Luna stated, throwing a last handful of dried leaves upon its base. "Are you?"

Ellie returned her gaze. "I am." Samael watched from the outskirts of the clearing. She noticed a look of concern cross the twisted features of the hag beside her. "Sister Luna, are *you?*" she asked, placing a gentle hand around her arm.

Luna offered a smile in return. "I am, Ellie. And I am proud of you." She took Ellie's hand. "You have learned so much in so little a time. You have seen both the bad and the good of what happens in my world; in *our* world," she emphasised, grasping Ellie's hand tighter. "You must always protect yourself and your allies, Ellie, as they are the ones who have protected you during this time of enlightenment. All beings which exist by the moonlight, whether it be witch, warlock, lycanthrope or vampire, should stand together against society. You are a beacon for them, Ellie. You will be the one looked upon to preserve our way of life for the rest of yours. Do not let our kind die. You are the one true being that can stand against any opposition and remain defiant. You are the leader of the dark masses. Be strong, my dear, be strong."

Ellie smiled and squeezed Luna's hand. "You have taught well, Luna, and given me the belief from which I can now draw strength. I have seen the ugliness of society, and I swear, with the Dark Lord as my witness, that I will do everything to preserve our kind and our way of life. Thank you."

She gave a humble, loving smile to Luna and felt her eyes brimming.

"Well, child, we must call upon the dark realm. I want you to summon the demon for yourself. You must recall that first night when the flame burned upon your finger, and recall the action you took to loft the flames in to the sky. Do you remember?" Ellie nodded. "Good. Then step toward the fire." Ellie released the hags hand and walked towards the flames. Luna recited the same words as she had done that first night. "Look at the fire, Ellie, and tell me what you see. Look deep, beyond the curtains of the flames, and tell me what you see. Open your mind, not your eyes."

Ellie stood defiant, staring deep into its burning aura. Within her mind's eye the demon appeared. Rage washed over her.

"I call upon you, and demand you appear!" A low groan bellowed from the forest. "Show yourself!"

"Ellie!" Luna snapped, "show respect!"

The ground trembled. Ellie looked about the forest, sensing creatures watching before actually seeing them. Hundreds of eyes twinkled in the darkness, reflecting the flames. Small, grotesque creatures groaning from the trees had surrounded the clearing. Many had horns. All had grotesque features, either squashed noses or twisted mouths.

Luna gasped. "Goblins! Demons!" she whittled. Unbeknown to Ellie this was turning to a sacrifice. Her blatant disrespect for the underworld had sealed her fate. "Ellie!"

"Leave her!" boomed a voice from the fire. Ellie gave a wry smile as she watched her tormentor rise from its pit. Clawed hands grasped the ground. Long, twisted horns emerged, and intense eyes which glared as they appeared. The demon pushed itself in to their world and roared, scattering the wildlife from the surrounding area. The audience of creatures gasped and giggled in a frenzied excitement. The demon shook its head and looked down at the woman who had challenged.

Luna hurried toward the fire. "My Lord-"

"I am not the Lord!" the demon spewed angrily. "I am the one you called upon to present this filth to him." The demon turned to Luna. "Leave, now! Your service is valuable and I wish you no harm."

Ellie turned to her mentor. "Go."

"Leave us," the demon growled.

"Luna," Samael begged from the treeline. Ellie watched Luna slowly retreat. "Hurry up!" he gasped. Luna looked back to Ellie. Slowly she began to shuffle away, her body rocking from one side to the other as she retreated. Ellie watched her vanish into the darkness of the forest but knew she would not disappear entirely.

"You have the audacity to challenge me!" the demon snarled, throwing its clawed palm towards Ellie. A wave of energy struck and thrust her to the ground. The creatures giggled and applauded from their vantage points. Ellie gasped, feeling the wind knocked from her as she lay upon the cold grass. "You are nothing more than an insignificant insect, a blemish on this world," the demon stated, raising its palm upwards. Ellie levitated from the forest floor. She lurched up, suspended in mid-air. An invisible vice clasped Ellie's throat. "You were not worthy of a place within the Dark Lord's masses back then, and you're not worthy now." The demon gritted its teeth. Ellie gasped as the pressure increased. "You will die for your insult, girl. I will drag you to the bowels of our realm and have you tortured and maimed for eternity. Your suffering will be legendary." Ellie choked and coughed. The demon leant forward and smiled. "You are weak and pathetic," it chuckled, taking pleasure in Ellie's discomfort. The minions around him giggled *en masse*. Ellie attempted to speak. The demon released the grasp around her throat. "What is it? What did you say?"

Ellie coughed. "That...was...exactly what...I wanted you...to...believe..."

The demon snarled. "Wha..."

A blast of energy caught the demon off guard. Ellie slumped to the ground. The demon lurched backwards from the fire. "What is this?" it screamed.

Ellie lifted her head to face the creature, her red eyes burning. Finally, the rage had been released. "Me," she replied, delighting in the surprise that crossed the demon's face.

"You? You!" Its clawed hands rose to retaliate.

Ellie thrust her palms forward, striking the beast with a powerful energy. She rose to her feet. The demon writhed and contorted in the flames. Ellie's right arm remained extended, as though holding the creature within her grasp. The beast struggled, filling the darkened forest with a hellacious scream. With her left hand Ellie circled her fingers and clenched her fist. The demon gasped. Ellie snarled and jolted it downward. The screams of rage turned to pain as the creature buckled with her pressure. Its horns contorted at Ellie's will and imagination, tearing from the beast's skull. Black liquid splattered in to the clearing.

"You go back to where you came from," Ellie growled, her voice no more than a whisper, but she knew the demon listened. "You go back to the realm from whence you came, and you give a message to every creature that dwells there."

"What? What is it that you ask of me?" the demon howled.

Blood seeped into the clearing. The demon groaned once more. "You know what to do." Ellie opened the gateway back to Hell, creating flames which erupted high into the night sky. The screams and cries from the souls damned within their realm wafted throughout the clearing as the fire raged higher. Ellie grinned. Across the beast's torso a series of lacerations appeared, some so deep that blood spilled from them. Together the injuries spelled two words. "Fear me," Ellie read to the beast. The fire roared upward and a host of demonic arms and claws emerged around their minion, clasping at its body. The demon writhed as the hands took hold, dragging it back to the realm of tortured souls. The flames burned greater as the damned returned the beast to its rightful place. Ellie watched the demon sink behind the flames until it vanished, rescued from her power by those of whom she sought to serve.

Ellie watched on a moment or so, noticing now the fire returned to the size it had been when Luna crafted it, flickering harmlessly as though nothing had happened. Returning to her consciousness came the sound of the small creatures surrounding the area. Ellie frowned. Blood and organs cascaded outwards as she destroyed them all with one, swift thought. Only then did Ellie notice her own, laboured breathing from the effort of her exertions, now catching up to her.

From the darkness Sister Luna and Samael emerged. They said nothing. Their expressions spoke louder than a thousand words. She knew, now. She knew that now was the time. Not only would she exact her vengeance on the society that sentenced her to death, but also on those who took young Azur from his mother. Now was her time, and she promised that the next time she spilled blood, it would be human.

The witches wandered silently through the forest, guided by the lights of a lantern and the accompanying fairies. The wind rattled between the branches as it gusted past the trees, their limbs clattering within the darkness. Ellie thought of nothing but revenge. Her mind swirled with dark thoughts as she wandered behind Luna, following the lights back to their home. To think, she once lived amongst those people, people who exchanged payment to allow a band of murderers loose within their town, which led to the callous death of a child. The thought was sickening. They should all be held accountable, each and every one of them.

Luna stopped ahead. Ellie returned from her thoughts instantly. "Do you hear that?" the hag asked, waving the lantern around in the darkness. The nervousness within her voice was unsettling to say the least, making Ellie anxious.

"Hear what?" she asked, following Luna's gaze. The wind settled, returning the forest to silence. From the distance, and very faintly, a wail emerged. It echoed from the depths, sorrowful and eerie as it drifted toward the travelling witches. "What-"

"Hush, Ellie! Listen!"

The anxiety Luna expressed was most unnerving, but Ellie did as she was asked. Remaining silent she listened, hearing the wail grow louder. The scream trailed off and diminished, as strangely as it had started. Luna continued to scour the forest. Ellie looked around, unsure exactly what to be looking for. One thing that was noticeable, though, was that the accompanying fairies had vanished from their side. Ellie turned back to Luna. Trees moaned as the wind past by them.

The wail pierced the darkness. It filled their ears with a terrible cry and screamed in to Ellie's mind. Overwhelming sensations of fear and sadness subdued her, forcing the witch to crouch and place hands across her ears.

"Be gone! Be gone!" Luna screamed, waving her hands erratically. The wail continued, long and woeful, until finally fading back to whence it came. The forest stood motionless for a moment. Luna cocked an ear and scoured the forest once more. "It is gone."

Ellie rose from the ground, her ears still ringing from the wail. "What was it?" she asked, having heard nothing like the scream in all her life.

Luna turned, lifting the lantern to illuminate them both. "A Banshee. The most feared spirit upon this world."

Ellie's stomach fluttered. "Why? Why is it so feared?"

"Because, my dear, the Banshee is a foreteller of death. It only makes its presence felt under the most extreme circumstance. The sorrowful nature of the scream warns any who hear it of forthcoming doom."

"Is it ours? Our doom being foretold?"

Luna shook her head slightly. "Not necessarily. Maybe, maybe not. It may be the death of someone we know, or one we will be involved in. One thing is certain, though, this is a warning. We will be involved in some way with Samael in the very near future."

***

Spring was coming to the forest. The night breeze appeared warmer, if only a little, than it had previously. Guided by the returning Fairies, Ellie returned to Luna's house. She was weary, the encounter with the demon had been exhausting, as had been the wailing Banshee.

Luna went on ahead. As Ellie reached the house, something clattered inside it, focusing her attention back to her mentor.

"Luna?" she asked, slowly walking towards the door.

"Ellie!" Luna screamed. Ellie's stomach turned. The fear in the scream echoed across the clearing.

"Luna!" Ellie shouted, raising her dress to run freely.

She burst through the door. In the dim light she found Luna stood motionless. The hood on her robe had fallen, revealing her wispy hair. A blade shimmered at her exposed throat. From behind, a hand pulled the hag's head, raising the prominent chin upward.

Ellie glared to the man holding the weapon.

"Ah, ah, ah," Stearne laughed, grinning manically from behind his hostage. "You try anything and I'll slit her throat."

"Found you," came a voice from the darkness.

"Ellie, look out!"

Trial

Flames roared in to the night sky. Panic swept throughout the town. Bodies trailed blood and flesh as they stumbled between the burning buildings. Heat from the fires burned Ellie's skin as she wandered through the town of Elkwood. Its people fled in all directions, running erratically from the carnage around them. Warm blood splatter across her face as an axe plunged in to the skull of a screaming woman. Ellie paid no attention and moved towards her mother, burning from her place in a damned fire. It was clear what had happened. Ellie believed her mother had been trialled for witchcraft. There was no sign of pain or torture. Ellie's mother simply looked on, her body charred and bleeding.

She stopped at the flames and watched as her mother appeared then vanished quickly within the inferno.

"Now," the body whispered from within the searing heat, "now you must awaken." Ellie attempted to speak. "Do not say a word," her mother interrupted, "go forth, know that I love you and that we will always be bonded through our craft. Awaken, Ellie, awaken and seek your vengeance."

Ellie jerked into consciousness, her breathing shallow and rapid. She attempted to move but found her hands bound. As consciousness returned fully she noticed they had been pulled behind her and tied round a large wooden support reaching from the floor to the roof of the barn in which she sat. After only a second or so realisation set in. She was back in Elkwood and had been taken prisoner. Her legs stretched out before her, across the ground as she sat with her back pushed against the wooden frame to which she had been secured. Then pain struck. A pain so immense she could not think. The cutting sensation within her head forced her to cry out.

"Painful?" came a voice from the recesses of the barn. Reverend Jones emerged, clasping his bible and crucifix. Ellie struggled but rendered useless by the rope. "You can struggle, you can fight, but it will be in vain. Witches have no power when they cannot focus." The sharpness cut through Ellie's skull once more. "It's useless, heathen. You have been bested by the Lord God almighty and will be returned to the Hell that spawned you."

"What have you done to me?" Ellie gasped as the pain eased momentarily.

Reverend Jones wandered over and squatted beside her. He smiled and flicked at her temple. The sharpness intensified and tears welled from her eyes. "Something so simple," he mused. "Master Hopkins devised this little trick a year or so ago in Ipswich. Two tacks nailed lightly into your temples. The pain is tremendous, keeping you from focusing on anything but the torture that you suffer. You can't create your spells unless you focus properly." Ellie's head screamed. "This will keep you in order until we are ready to take you."

"Where?"

Jones grunted. "To the King." From outside the barn Ellie heard the sound of jeering. "It's your friend," he informed her as the pain returned. "She's about to burn."

"No," Ellie whispered. Whenever she gained composure the shredding sensation returned.

"I've told you, it's useless. Accept your fate, witch."

Sister Luna stood high into the overcast sky, bound within a cluster of dried branches and twigs. Mayor Randall led a group of townsfolk bearing flames. She had been beaten and judged, and the ache of her beating throbbed throughout her frail body. She was subjected to the same torture as Ellie. Two tacks protruded from her temple to stop her from casting her evil spells on those who judged her.

Matthew Hopkins looked up to his prize. "Now is the time, my good people," he began, addressing the mass of bodies surrounding him. "After years of poverty in your township you may now put to rest your fears and return to Hell the one who caused them!" The town cheered. Hopkins bowed to Mayor Randall and gestured with his hand towards the accused.

Randall snarled at Luna. "This is for everything you have cursed our town with, you wretched old hag! Burn! Burn in Hell!" He threw the flame into the branches and gestured with a swing of his arm for the others to do the same. The crowd intensified as the branches lighted and the flames merged to one.

The heat caressed her lower body. Luna hung limply. She heard the taunts. Witch! Heathen! The debris popped as the flames grew stronger.

Slowly Luna looked towards the crowd. "Ellie," she whispered.

"Luna," Ellie cried from the barn, sensing the dismay and terror her mentor was suffering. Ellie struggled to free herself once more but pain surged from her temples.

"She will come for you," Luna shouted to the masses. "She will come for you! All of you!" The townsfolk laughed. Pulsing heat flickered across her toes. It tormented and teased as it appeared and vanished, each pulse becoming stronger as the flames festered below. The heat crept along her legs. "She will kill you all!" The stinging sensation deepened and became unbearable . The pain became sharper and sharper until she screamed, throwing her haggard face up to the skies. It grew stronger and moved upwards to her thighs. The shawl she wore ignited. The wood crackled as the flames spread. Smoke stung her eyes. Sweat cascaded from her pores. Beneath the shawl her skin charred. It oozed and bled as the flames attacked relentlessly. Luna sobbed as the smell of her own, cooking flesh filled her nostrils.

"No!" Ellie screamed, wriggling furiously against the rope, ignoring the first pain that stabbed at her. The second sliced through more intensely causing her to scream. Tears trickled from her eyes. "Luna!"

The shawl was burnt against Luna's skin. She cried out as the flames burned hotter. The more she screamed the greater they became. Fire distorted her vision before heat forced her eyes to close, their lids burning away. Luna opened her mouth one final time. Blood poured. "She will kill you all! None of you are safe! None of you have known a power like hers! She will avenge my death, and those who you have slaughtered before me! You will all die! All of you!"

The crowd fell silent as Luna launched in to a hysterical, evil cackle, spewing blood high in the air as she laughed in torment. Her intestines boiled. Still she cackled. Still she laughed. Randall looked to Hopkins. Reverend Thomas whispered a silent prayer. The fire roared and Luna's cackle turned to a scream. She screamed and screamed as the flames roasted her body, until finally she fell silent. The flames continued to roar. The townsfolk stood hushed.

"Luna," Ellie whispered, her tears intensifying her pain.

Hopkins turned to the people of Elkwood. He stood prominently against the fire that ravaged the witch's body. "Good people," he began, raising a hand to make sure he had their attention. "Now is the time. Now we must strike, to ensure your town survives."

"What are you saying?" Randall snapped angrily.

"Mayor, good people, this witch is dead, the witch that has plagued you for so many years. We have her pupil in our custody whom we will take with us back to London to be examined by the King's good physicians. You are no longer at threat from the witch's curse. But, there are still some who lurk within this forest which may cause you concern."

153

"The lycanthropes!" Daniel shouted. He was standing with his arms folded, beside Lucian and behind the townsfolk.

"Thank you, Master Wade. Yes, the werewolves," Hopkins said, gaining the people's attention again. "Now, there is no full moon for many, many days. There is no chance of them changing to their primal form. If we should strike now, and strike quickly, we can eliminate the threat they pose to you good people and ensure that the safety of your town is guaranteed."

"And just how much will this cost us, Master Hopkins? You were not too keen on this idea a week ago," Mian asked from the recesses of the crowd.

"My good man, much has changed since that meeting. It will cost you nothing but a letter of recommendation to the King, signed from your good Mayor."

"Do it!" a man shouted.

"Yes!" came another.

The townsfolk began speaking in Hopkins' favour.

"Yes! Yes!"

"Master Hopkins," Randall said, taking grip of his arm, "consider it done."

The people cheered.

"In that case, make sure all men bring a weapon. Bring pitchforks and spades. Bring tools and knives. It matters not how you attack a lycanthrope during the daylight hours, it will die as any other human will."

Hopkins noticed a strange noise emerging behind the crowd. From the empty street the hooded executioner appeared, dragging his silver-tipped axe across the ground.

For the first time since the arrival of Hopkins and his company the townsfolk felt optimistic. Now he would lead them in one final push against the lycanthropes dwelling in the forest. He would lead them to vanquish the evils of the Earth and leave them to exist in peace. The township finally trusted and believed the Witchfinder, and were about to follow his company into battle, and to the ends of the Earth if he so desired.

Commotion swept past the barn where Ellie wept. The pain she suffered and the loss of her friend had resigned her to defeat. She rested upright against the wooden support, her hair matted against sodden cheeks. It had been blood that trickled from the tacks embedded in her temples, and not sweat as she once believed. Her dirty cotton dress was now stained red with drops and spatters of the liquid. Her eyes closed but she sensed a presence standing over. Slowly she looked up, as quickly as the pain would allow, and saw the caped figure of Matthew Hopkins smiling down.

"My dear, it is almost over," he explained in his distinctive voice. "I will lead these people in to the forest to destroy those filthy creatures that thrive by the moon, and then I will return to this wretched, godforsaken town." He stooped down to the injured woman. "And when I do, you will be bound and taken to London where you will undergo torture in the name of science. Once the physicians have had their way with you, you will be returned to me for disposal, and I will make sure you are disposed of in the most brutal manner necessary. You have been a thorn in my side unlike any other, and I will take much pleasure in your pain." Hopkins looked up to Reverend Jones. "But until then I will leave you in the capable hands of our good Reverend whilst we hunt down and destroy the wolves. Until I return," Hopkins stood swiftly and tipped his hat to the clergyman.

Jones made the sign of the holy cross. "Go, with the Lord's blessing."

"Indeed I shall," Hopkins replied, patting his comrade. The Witchfinder took a last look over his shoulder to Ellie and left the barn.

The commotion took a time to settle as the townspeople gathered their weapons together, but as the late afternoon light showed signs of dwindling they amassed together under the leadership of their new saviour.

Hopkins gave a rallying speech that Ellie could not quite hear from inside the barn, but recognised the cheers of the people amongst whom she once lived, and knew that along with John Stearne, Daniel Wade and Lucian, Hopkins's cull of the lycanthropes was about to begin.

Conflict

Wagner sensed a change in the atmosphere. It was as palpable as the sun itself. Agnieszka emerged by his side as he peered out into the trees. "Do you sense that?" he asked his daughter, lifting his nose to take the air.

Agnieszka felt it too. The air felt different. The sky looked different. All about them the winds of change swept through the forest. "Yes. I can hear something. It sounds large but I cannot make sense of it."

Wagner turned his head sideways and lifted his ear to the air. There; the distinctive sound of crowds. Shouting and screaming drifted between the leaves. "Humans," Wagner replied.

Agnieszka frowned. "Something is wrong. Something is very wrong," she whispered, closing her eyes, "they express much anger."

"Indeed." Wagner's anxiety increased with each heartbeat. He turned to see his community gather about them, sensing the change within the forest. Something moved in the distance.

"There! Do you see it?" a voice shouted.

From the depths of the trees a vast mass of people emerged, closing in on their position. They charged relentlessly, bearing weapons and flames. At their head ran Lucian and Wade.

"Oh no," Agnieszka whispered.

"Run! Run!" Wagner screamed to his people.

Without a second's hesitation the lycanthropes began fleeing their home. Women grabbed children. Men pushed women in the direction of escape. The forest filled with the terrified screams of women and the cries of children.

"Wagner!" a comrade shouted across the clearing. Wagner looked across and saw him beckon. Already the forest had been flooded with the escaping werewolves. They parted like water around the tree trunks and out beyond sight.

157

"There they are!" Lucian shouted as his followers approached the lycanthrope community. All clasped weapons with which to destroy the werewolves; spades, pitchforks, scythes, knives, anything that could be used to take the life of another. Fear had turned to anger as the townsmen sought to end the threat to their community once and for all. With the hag destroyed, a witch safely subdued back in the town and a group of men seasoned in destroying the paranormal, these men no longer feared the creatures of the forest.

Wade darted to the left and stopped beside an oak tree, removing the crossbow from his shoulder.

Lucian unsheathed his rapier as they approached the escaping werewolves. "Slaughter them! All of them!" he ordered as they left the trees and stormed in to the clearing.

An escaping lycanthrope fell from an arrow aimed by Wade. A strong male launched an attack at Lucian as the townsmen surged past and engaged with those standing against the attack. Lucian ducked as a barrage of punches flew towards him. The hunter swirled his rapier and flashed it down towards his attacker. The lycanthrope grasped his arm as the weapon plunged downward. Lucian, momentarily distracted, took a mighty blow to the face which knocked him back, into the fighting crowds. The rapier fell to the ground and vanished from sight within the melee.

Wade shot down a female and watched her writhe. Men carrying torches thrust them inside the structures about them, bathing the battlefield in an orange glow. Lycanthropes fell to the ground, clubbed and battered mercilessly by their attackers.

Lucian charged towards a lycanthrope and engaged a battle of fists. Each traded blows with the other. The lycanthrope fell backward with the sheer force of a strike by Lucian, his head jerking backwards as he tumbled down.

"Kill them!" Lucian screamed before charging through the air, slamming his knees down on his opponent. The hulking figure lurched upwards with the impact and grabbed the hunter by the throat. Lucian clasped at the hand squeezing his windpipe. The lycanthrope rose to his feet, clutching Lucian. Once upright, he smashed his forehead on the bridge of Lucian's nose before throwing him to the ground. Lucian shook his head in an attempt to clear the fuzziness and ringing. Under his scarf the warm trickle of blood oozed from his nostrils.

"Come on!" the lycanthrope screamed, punching at his own chest. Lucian pushed himself up and locked eyes with the enemy. They glared at one another through the chaos, each intent on destroying the other.

From across the distance the Witchfinder approached the battle. "Rid these lands," he said quietly as his horse cantered closer.

Wagner smashed away his attackers as they bore down upon him. He snatched weapons and used them against their former owners. His clothing became splattered with the blood and mud. All around him death took hold. With so many bodies lurching and fighting it was difficult to distinguish between friend and enemy. From nowhere an attacker leapt from behind. Wagner swayed and grabbed blindly at the hair of his enemy. Heavy blows began jarring his head as the lycanthrope found a handful of hair and pulled. A scream filled his ears and momentarily the grip around him eased. Wagner clutched the hair tighter and dropped forward, launching the attacker over his shoulder. A body fell on the grass. Wagner scowled and smashed his foot down upon its skull, feeling the nose implode under foot. Gasping for breath Wagner looked on the carnage with dismay. Flames came from the homes of his people. Smoke billowed in to the air, filling the lungs and stinging the eyes of those battling within it.

"Father!" Wagner's daughter waded tearfully between the bodies.

"Go!" he ordered angrily, pushing her away.

"Father?"

"Go! I will stay! I must protect our home and our people!"

"What? That is madness!"

Wagner glared at her. "Then madness it is! Go! Now!"

Without uttering a further word the two embraced before Agnieszka turned away from the battle. She joined a large group lycanthropes fleeing in her direction. A dreadful feeling passed as he realised this might be the last time he would ever lay eyes upon his daughter. Wagner raged at the thought and turned toward an aggressor bearing a shovel. He growled and launched to the battle.

Ellie opened her eyes. She had been left in silence. Pain attacked again, causing her to sigh and wince.

"Awake, are we?" Reverend Jones asked from his perch on a bale of hay.

"How long?" Ellie croaked, sensing he had not left during the time she was unconscious.

"How long, what?"

Ellie grimaced. The pain was unbearable. "Sleep?" she asked hesitantly, unable to mutter anything more.

Jones shrugged. "Not long. A matter of minutes, maybe?"

Ellie sighed. Her rage had vanished. Everything she had learnt, everything she had worked towards had failed. Luna was dead, her remains still smouldering in the remnants of Hopkins' fire. The lycanthropes were to be hunted and slaughtered by the Witchfinder's company and the residents of Elkwood. Maybe she wasn't as powerful as she had been led to believe. Maybe this wasn't about her after all.

Reverend Jones stood and made his way across to the slumped body bound to the barn support. Ellie looked up as he stared down at her, grinning. In the rafters behind him she noticed movement. Something was moving. As the pain came and went a shade of white nestled quietly above the clergyman. She realised, it wasn't a shade at all, it was a bird. Cyrius perched high up inside the loft, hidden from immediate view, peering back with great interest.

"Sooner or later the error of your way was bound to catch up with you," Jones began. Ellie turned sideways as the pain surged once more. The barn door hung slightly open. Against the light streaming in from outside stood the silhouette of an animal. She recognised the creature. Streak looked at his mistress and dashed silently inside the structure, out of view. Jones noticed her focus in a different direction and followed the gaze to the barn door for himself. Ellie prayed that her animals remained hidden. Reverend Jones studied the gloomy structure. Scouring the barn one last time he turned back to his prisoner. "The dark arts will always lead you to this outcome. Your lord does not care for you. He does not protect you as our Lord God Almighty protects his own. I have been a part of Hopkins' company for many a year and still I stand in front of you now, after all the battles I have endured. The Lord God Almighty protects those within his service, and I serve him very well."

The Reverend's expression changed. His eyes shifted upwards. Gurgles and gasps emerged from his throat. The clergyman shook and quivered. The Bible fell from his grasp and down to the straw-littered floor. The skin around his face tightened against the bone. Ridges emerged as though the skin was shrinking. His clothing hung limply from his frame. Dust spewed from his mouth. The Reverend rotted to a greying skeleton. Dust expelled from every orifice as he quaked uncontrollably. He shuddered one final time before falling to the ground, expelling a further mass of chalky cloud into the air. Nothing more than bones existed inside the bundle of clothes that Reverend Jones once wore.

"I can't stand to see an unfair fight," came a familiar voice in Ellie's ear. Cyrius swooped down and rested beside her as Streak dashed from his cover to join them. Samael came into view and knelt in front of her. Ellie grimaced as another wave of pain emanated.

"Don't move. If I touch you, you're lost." Ellie gave a gentle nod to confirm she understood. "This is going to hurt."

"Do it," she whispered.

Samael delicately pinched the tacks embedded in Ellie's temple. She winced. "I said don't move!" he snapped, pinching the tacks again. Quickly he took hold and pulled them free. Ellie screamed and rolled forward. Blood poured from the wounds. The pain was still there. "Ellie, look at me," Samael ordered. "Look at me!"

Ellie gazed at his familiar features. He still wore the strange headwear which rested awkwardly on his head. Samael waved a hand across her face, quick as a flash. The pain disappeared. Ellie awoke, vibrant and energetic. "What did you do?" she asked as he stood upright, adjusting his top hat.

He smiled back at her. "I don't just take lives. You know, sometimes I can restore them." Ellie looked around. Her Familiars stood loyally by her side. "Right, that's the first and last time I will help you, my lady," Samael said, pulling at his fingerless gloves to make them sit more comfortably. "You've got your mind back. You have your belief. Out there you have an entire community of lycanthropes about to be butchered. I know because I'm on my way there now to collect all of their souls. It's up to you to save them, or you can leave them to be destroyed, it's your choice."

"My decision has already been made. Streak," she ordered, gesturing with her head to the hands still bound behind her. Streak trotted round to the rope and began to chew. "You will get your fifty souls and you will get them before the evening is through."

Samael clapped his hands together. "So go and do it."

Ellie pulled against the ropes and snapped the binding that the fox had chewed. Standing upright she brushed debris from her blood-stained dress and looked toward her rescuer.

"Yes," he said quietly, nodding his head gently as he did so, "I can feel it in the air. I can feel it all around us now."

"What?" Ellie asked as she prepared to leave.

Samael's eyes widened. "Death."

Wagner battered his attacker with a clenched fist. The attacker thrust the shovel at his head as he tumbled back, before losing balance with the ferocity of the strike, and veered sideways. Wagner lurched across and took hold of his throat. With a swift, powerful movement the lycanthrope ripped a gash and cheered across the battlefield, raising the flesh aloft in victory. The man stumbled and swayed through the carnage, clutching at his throat and gasping for breath before vanishing from view. A lycanthrope jumped past and tackled a farmer wielding a pitchfork, smashing him sideways to the ground. Wagner spun and watched as his comrade beat and pounded his victim. The lycanthropes knew that now, out here on this battlefield, it was kill or be killed. Wagner engaged his senses and leapt to battle again.

Agnieszka sprinted between the trees as she fled from the battle, jeering those around her to run faster. Some laboured as their attackers gave chase. The anger from their pursuers bellowed across the forest. People screamed. Lycanthropes fell.

Lucian smashed the jaw of his opponent. The lycanthrope jerked sideways and snarled, swinging a larger fist in retaliation. Lucian battered away with his forearm and struck across the cheekbone with an elbow. Kicking his attacker, Lucian turned to find his rapier. Madness had engulfed the forest. Everywhere he peered, people fought against people. Blood seared in to the air and splashed across the terrain. Lucian could not see the ground through fallen bodies and blood-stained fighters. Then, between vying feet and jostling people, he noticed his weapon resting in a pile of long grass a few feet away. He dived across, rolled over the ground and took the blade in one clean tumble. Forgetting the nearby lycanthropes fighting beside him he turned to the one with whom he was battling. The lycanthrope screamed and charged towards the hunter, barging bodies from his path with immense power. Lucian planted a foot in to the earth and launched himself from the ground, swinging the rapier in mid-air. The blade flashed down, severing the arm of his charging attacker. The Lycanthrope began to scream as the infection seeped into his body from the cut. Lucian turned from his enemy knowing his fate had been sealed. Throughout the deafening roar and clattering weapons that surrounded the area, he focused on the nearest lycanthrope and launched in to the next battle, his rapier shimmering in the poor light as he did so.

The barn door exploded in to a million shards and scattered across the tight street in which it was housed. Ellie strode out from its confines, no longer bound or subdued. A light patter of rain began to fall, cooling her exposed skin. She looked around at Elkwood, at the town she had come to know so well, and from which she had been expelled. The streets lay empty. The rain rattled the buildings. The women and children were hiding away, ignorant of the witch's presence. A pig grunted in its pen across the way. A noise gained her attention briefly. Turning to her left Ellie looked down the tiny street toward the square. Smoke wafted upwards still, visible above the roofs of the houses that separated them. For a moment she considered venturing to the fire where Luna's remnants roasted, thinking that maybe there was a chance she could be saved, but the connection she gained with Luna was lost. There was no way of saving the witch now. Her mentor, her friend, was gone. She was gone, and there was nothing now that could be done to bring her back.

"Ellie?"

Ellie froze. A familiar voice returned her to her senses. She turned in the direction from which it came. There, ragged and evidently heartbroken stood her distraught father. His eyes were stained red by the constant shedding of tears. His face showed stress and turmoil. He stood in the same clothes that he had worn when condemning his own daughter as a witch.

"Ellie? Ellie, I am so sorry. I am-"

"Hush," Ellie replied, raising a finger to silence the broken figure. Ted took notice and stopped talking. A new emotion emerged which she had never experienced in all the years that they had shared together. No longer did she look upon him with love and affection. She felt anger. Anger and rage. Ellie gritted her teeth and turned away.

"Ellie, I…"

"I know, father, I know. You were only doing what you felt best. What was right for me, correct?"

"Ellie you know it is the truth," he replied.

"A quick and peaceful death, is that what you wanted?"

"I did not want you dead at all, Ellie. I'd known of your curse for years and did my very best to keep it hidden from these damned people. I never wanted this, never."

"Then why did you condemn me?" she screamed, turning back with a snarl on her face.

"Because they were going to kill you! No matter who accused this or who accused that, they were killing you regardless. Don't you see? I didn't want you tortured at the stake like those who had been accused previously. I didn't want you tortured like…" Ted drew a shallow breath. "I didn't want you tortured like your mother."

Deep down Ellie had known it. A vision came of her mother burning within a fire, spewing blood as she laughed and tormented those inside the dream world.

"You inherited your gift from her, and in turn I did everything to keep it hidden from them. From all of them. You had nightmares that shook the buildings wherever you lay. In the end your gift was so powerful I simply could not hide it any longer."

"Is that what you call it, father? You call it a gift? Let me tell you what I call it. I call it a curse, along with every other woman who stood accused as I did! Why? Why kill these women just because they were different? Most of them did nothing to harm the community in which we lived. Did picking an herb or owning a pet cause any such harm to the peasants living within this damned town? Did that give the Mayor any right to destroy all of those women?"

Ted held his palms towards her. "Ellie, not me. I had nothing to do with the trials of the accused."

"No, you didn't," she said quietly as tears rolled down her cheek, "but you did when I stood there, accused of witchcraft."

"Ellie."

"No! I was beaten, I was bound and I was left tied to a tree in the middle of nowhere to die by the elements! Do you know how painful that was? Do you know how much suffering I endured that night?"

"I did what I thought was best for you."

"You did nothing!" Ellie screamed, clenching her fists so tight they shook beside her. Ted jerked upright. "You did nothing to help me, your own daughter, nor even your own wife when she was judged and executed!"

"Ellie!" he gasped.

Ellie's rage flooded through her veins. "You stood by in the crowd and watched on as your true love and your own flesh and blood stood accused! You did nothing as they were tortured and murdered in the name of the King of England and the Lord God Almighty!"

"Ellie!"

Ellie trembled as rage took hold. She lifted her head upwards and reached out a hand. Ted levitated into the air. Anger coursed throughout Ellie's body. Her clenched fist shook with tension. Ted gasped. Blood exploded from his mouth and nose, soiling his tunic and trousers. "I judge you now, as you did me, father, as a coward and a liar, hiding behind the work of your pathetic God." Ted howled. His left leg buckled at the knee and snapped completely. "I am a heretic, too powerful to be governed by your God or even by Satan himself. I find you guilty of treachery to your own wife and daughter, and sentence you to death." Ellie's eyes grew red as her ability grew stronger. Wind gusted about her body. Debris from the empty street plastered against her dress.

"Ellie…"

"The daughter you once knew and raised does not exist anymore. All that exists is anger and suffering. I have no compassion. I have no remorse. I am the one who will even the odds against mankind. I am the witch who will fight for those who dwell in darkness. The world of man will know of my power. I am death incarnate to this natural world. Fear me!" Ted's body exploded. Blood mixed with rain as his innards slopped to the ground. Ellie looked skywards and closed her eyes, stretching out her arms and reaching to the heavens as the morbid rain poured down on top of her. The ground quaked beneath her feet as she shook with an overwhelming rage. Her eyes burned. She recalled Hopkins and his company, remembering the townspeople flooding to the woods to find Wagner and his defenceless people.

She remembered Azur and how powerless they had all been to save him. The lycanthropes were out there, unable to protect themselves against the Witchfinder, his makeshift army and their deadly weapons. Her brethren were being slaughtered, defenceless and afraid. Ellie screamed again, her shriek echoing like the Banshee throughout the town and forest around. Birds flooded from the trees. Lightning flashed from her hands and in to the overcast sky as she channelled her power to maximum capability.

The element crackled as it flickered and danced upwards in to the clouds. The rain thundered down and pelted her body. Her wail rattled and shattered nearby windows as her anger surged. Glass exploded in every direction. Lamps smashed allowing fires to escape their confines. Wagner, Agnieszka, all of them battled an enemy they simply could not defeat. All of them would certainly die. The rain fell more prominent. Ellie ceased screaming. Lightning roared from her palms and flashed in to the rainclouds, leaving her motionless, her head tipped back and arms outstretched. Streak and Cyrius emerged at her side. Ellie dropped her head. She closed her eyes. From the darkness of her inner consciousness she created a moon within her mind, a moon so bright and vivid it hung brightly in a clear, cloudless sky, brighter than any moon that had ever glowed before. Clouds flew past its intense aura. Ellie heard a long, mythical howl emerge from the darkness. Through the howls and snarls a silhouette launched, its eyes amber, its jaws agape.

Wagner twitched. He stopped in the midst of the fight as he felt a surreal sensation take over his body. Muscles began to pull in various directions. About him his comrades contorted on the battlefield. The townsmen stopped their onslaught, noticing the pain to which their foes had fallen. All about them the lycanthropes fell to the sodden ground, twisting and shaking. Wagner knew this ferocious pain as it took hold of his body and sent him falling.

Agnieszka slumped to the mud, believing herself injured until recognising the pain as the one which appeared with the full moon. About her the others fell, some beginning their transformation. Muzzles appeared in place of noses. Fur emerged on top of skin. Agnieszka's nose broke. Pain ripped across her skull. A face appeared in her mind, the face of a young witch whom she knew very well.

Lucian swung his blade. Around his enemies fell. He looked on from beneath the rim of his headwear as the enemy. Anxiety surged through his body. The human forms began morphing. Bones broke. Claws appeared. "They're changing! They're changing!" Lucian bellowed from the battle. He turned back to face Hopkins.

Hopkins looked out across the chaos. The rain distorted his vision. Within the body-littered forest he saw his enemies morphing, all of whom filled the air with harsh, tortuous screams and primal howls as their transformation took effect. They were shifting without the effects of the full moon. His surprise turned to nervousness. "Kill them!" he shouted, his voice panic stricken. "Kill them now!" Hopkins turned his attention to Wade. "Daniel! Shoot them! Shoot them!"

Daniel took aim and fired an arrow into a contorting body. Lucian plunged his rapier into the changeling closest to him.

Throughout the forest wolves emerged, snorting and growling as they turned on and approached their aggressors. No longer were they restricted to their human bodies. Now, they had changed to the beasts that the Witchfinder and his army had set out to destroy. Panic engulfed the simpletons. One screamed and fled. Another followed. Quickly, the superstitious townsmen turned from battle and fled around the trees, rushing past Hopkins and Wade in a hectic stampede. Wade squinted through his crossbow from its firing position as the terrified mob charged into view.

"What are you doing?" Hopkins screamed at the bodies rushing around his horse and back to town.

Lucian stood alone beneath the falling rain as a pack of werewolves paced towards him, snorting plumes of mist in to the cold air. Saliva hung from their jaws. Their chests thudded and rumbled malevolently as they slowly stalked toward him. Lucian placed the tip of his rapier in the damp earth and lightly drew a line ahead of him with the tip. He span the handle in his palm, slicing the air with a rush of wind that whistled to his ears. As the hulking entity's approached, blocking most of the background foliage from his view, Lucian clasped his weapon with both hands and stood firm. The rain dripped from his hat's rim. His eyes darted from each wolf to the other in rapid succession, knowing that one would lunge any second.

Ellie opened her eyes. The rain saturated her hair and plastered it against her blood-drenched clothing. It glided and danced within the breeze surrounding her. Thunder bellowed across the skies. From somewhere across another plain she felt the presence of every witch and warlock murdered for practicing the dark arts. Thousands of entity's made themselves known to her. They flowed within her blood and existed in her mind. Women and men executed for simply existing, killed for being different or holding a different belief. Killed for not conforming. Ellie shivered as goosebumps shimmered across her body. Now she felt her power stronger than it had ever been before. It rippled throughout her being, just as Luna had told her. Finally, she realised that this was her fate all along. She was destined to be a witch from the moment she was born. Ellie focused on exacting revenge. She focused on killing all of those who persecuted her, and smiled. She was death incarnate, and they would all be judged and executed for their sins. Her palms turned outwards. "Now is the time," she whispered in to the storm.

With burning eyes and a terrible rage that would only be quelled with revenge, the witch darted from Elkwood and into the surrounding trees.

Lucian swung his rapier, slicing the lycanthropes as they bore down upon him one after the other. The blade pierced their flesh and killed them instantly.

Wade fired his silver-tipped arrows in to the melee of advancing wolves and terrified townsmen.

"Kill them!" Hopkins screamed, drawing a small pistol from beneath his cape. He took aim at a wolf and fired, hitting the beast in the forehead. The executioner wielded his axe on an attacking lycanthrope, slicing it clean in half. Both he and Lucian stood together as the relentless wave of beasts launched into battle.

Ellie glided across the grass. Cyrius twinkled and ascended into the sky. Streak darted from her side into long undergrowth. She felt no exhaustion as she sprinted through the forest, for she was consumed with rage for Hopkins and his comrades. She sped through ferns and shrubs which left damp patches on her soiled dress. She focused only on one thing; death. She felt the adrenalin and excitement of her power: everything she had once feared was now a source of strength. The once timid town girl had evolved to a harbinger of death. The rain pattered against her face. She felt vibrant. She felt alive. She felt Sister Luna lurking somewhere in the atmosphere, willing her to shed blood and fulfil her debt to Samael. In her mind she heard the hag cackling. All of her persecutors would fall by her hand, in payment for their atrocities against Luna and young Azur. Her excitement intensified: she was drawing close, she could feel it.

Lucian fell to the ground. Wade took aim and struck a wolf pouncing upon his comrade, thrusting it into the air. Wolves flooded from the darkened forest. The more that fell, the more emerged.

Hopkins noticed how intent the wolves had become in targeting his men. He smiled contently and placed his pistol back from where it had been drawn. Pulling back on the reigns of his horse he turned from the battle and cantered away, not once considering the safety of his company or having any interest in assisting them.

"Hey!" Wade shouted above the thunder, noticing his leader's departure from the battlefield. "Master Hopkins! Sir!" Hopkins paid no attention. He steered his horse around an oak and out in to a small pocket of clear grass. Quickly Wade loaded his crossbow and took aim. "You damned cowardly bastard!" he muttered, finding Hopkins in the sights of his crossbow. But the shot was not clear; foliage intermittently obscured his view as Hopkins rode between the trees. Then a brief gap appeared. Wade squeezed the trigger.

Amber eyes appeared in his sight before an impact smashed the hunter from his feet and through the air. Wade struck a trunk and slumped to the ground. He placed a hand to his side where he had been hit and felt blood seep between his fingers.

Three wolves stalked him from different directions, each converging on the tree against which he was leaning. Their snarls could be heard above the hissing rain. Frantically, Daniel patted at the ground in search of the crossbow he had dropped. He had no idea that these lycanthropes had crossed paths with him once before. The trio had witnessed him stalk a juvenile and watched as the boy was taken by the very hands that now scoured the soaking grass. Wade panicked as the wolves came to a standstill. He couldn't reach his crossbow. He whimpered as the snarling muzzles, sharp fangs and dripping jaws of the animals stared at him. The lycanthropes looked at each other in turn. One pointed its muzzle towards the fallen hunter. The growl grew deeper. Wade became frantic, fumbling for a weapon that was no longer there. The beast roared. Wade screamed. Blood splashed against the bark as Azur's mother took her revenge.

Heretic

Ellie saw them. The aggressors retreated from the battle. The spell had worked. "Forty nine remaining," a voice shouted to her through the driving rain. She turned to see Samael running alongside. He darted between the evergreens and vanished. The townspeople approached. The burning shade of red returned to her eyes. The people approached her. Those who had accused and demanded her death now fled in fear of their own lives. Through the darkening atmosphere and driving rain her eyes burned as brightly as the flames of a stake fire feasting upon the body of an accused. Above, the ancient trees began contorting. They creaked as they shifted and swayed, their leaves twisting down to the forest floor. Protruding from the leaves were a cluster of spikes hanging from the sky, formed from branches that Ellie's mind created. The group of men approaching tried to pass on either side. She flicked her eyebrows. They hurled upwards with the force and impaled on the spikes, squirming upon the foliage now soaked in their blood. As they screamed the canopies swayed once more, the trees now alive as they clutched their prey. Ellie delighted in their torture. The captives bellowed through the rainfall. Blood rained from the trees. The cries of the townsmen echoed through the forest as they were decapitated, each appendage falling to the forest floor.

The rain pounded the witch. Her skin turned pale. Blue veins emerged on her neck and cheeks as self-belief now permeated her being. She thrust her hands towards the next wave of fleeing attackers trying to escape the lycanthropes. Her mind sliced them all, severing their torsos in one, clean cut. The bodies flopped to the ground, spilling their crimson contents across the vegetation. Ellie dashed onward. Townspeople she knew and recognised exploded at will, filling the air with body parts as her retribution continued. Arms, legs and torsos fell in her wake as she sprinted, her hair and clothing now matted with a mixture of rain, blood and flesh.

"That's it! That's it! Believe, Ellie! Believe!"

From a great distance the disembodied voice of Sister Luna encouraged her. Ellie could not say whether the voice was in the forest or her mind, but hearing the witch only spurred her onward. Tree branches grabbed the townsmen, binding them against bark, restricting movement and constricting them. A group of men launched high into the rainclouds. Lightning flashed across the sky, exploding their bodies with a powerful thrash. Still she ran on, searching for the one who had caused all this, the Witchfinder General.

The executioner flung his axe towards a group of oncoming wolves. The lycanthropes leapt toward their target, knocking him to the ground. His body became immobile as they engulfed the gigantic man within their pack. His clothing tore, then flesh, and screamed as his gut ripped apart. A terrible pain unlike any he had ever known engulfed his body as his intestines were mauled by the feasting wolves.

Lucian stopped. He noticed now how heavily the rain fell. About him lay the bodies of men and women, some who had returned to their human form, some who had accompanied him to battle. Human debris littered the forest. The lycanthropes had vanished. Exhausted, Lucian listened to the heavy pattering of the rain against the leaves and sighed before dropping his rapier. Blood trickled from his fingers. Reaching up he took hold of his hat brim and removed it, dropping it beside the weapon. His long, dark hair immediately soaked as the rain cascaded down on top of him. Reaching behind his neck he untied the knot in the scarf. The hunter stood alone in the rain, the sole human survivor on the battlefield. He turned to survey the damage as the rain trickled down his scarred face, the face he had always kept hidden away. The right cheek was but strings of lacerated flesh where it had melted years before. The wetness on his skin brought with it a brief memory of the rainy night when a witch he trialled sprung from the fire and dragged him briefly inside.

"Hopkins!" he bellowed in to the descending darkness. "Hopkins, you coward! Show yourself!"

Ellie continued to harbour death. The townspeople died gratuitously as she passed them, all felled to her heinous will. The body count rose but she had no interest in how many had been slaughtered. Ahead of her was Hopkins. The Witchfinder cantered slowly through the rain heading steadily in her direction. Now she could commit the atrocities against the man whom she wanted to the most.

A flash of white light blinded her vision. Pain surged through her skull. Ellie fell heavily upon her back, looking up into the falling rain. Her jaw ached so badly she almost cried. A sensation of light-headedness buzzed within her brain. She was struck by something as she passed a tree. The metallic taste of blood filled her mouth. From beyond the double vision she heard a laugh. It belonged to someone that she remembered from her trial. The chuckle grew louder as it grew nearer.

"You stupid fool! Did you honestly believe we wouldn't factor you in to all this?"

John Stearne appeared above Ellie, his thick beard twisting upward as he grinned. "You're all the same, the lot of you. Think you're so special, don't you? You think that you're the one who can finally stop the Witchfinder General and his company of despicable hunters, eh?" He fumbled inside his pocket and squatted down beside Ellie's head. Ellie looked groggily at the two tacks he held out. Dread washed over her.

"No. No, not this," she whispered wearily.

"We've heard it all before," Stearne began, "and you know what? You filthy wretches are all the same. None of you will ever thrive;

you're all too stupid. We will continue to hunt you until you are all dead, each and every one of you." Ellie lay too disorientated to create any spell. Her mind was incoherent.

"Hurry up! Get it done!" Hopkins snapped from across the way.

"Right you are, sir," Stearne replied. He turned his attention back to Ellie and reached down in the grass, grabbing the hefty stone with which he had attacked her. "It ain't a hammer but it'll do."

Ellie tensed. "No, please, no."

Stearne thrust her head sideways. Her right cheek rolled over the soggy grass. Between thumb and forefinger he held a tack. The sharp point scratched Ellie's temple as he held it in place. "Be a shame if it goes in too deep," he mused, drawing back the stone ready to strike. Ellie drew one last breath and grimaced, anticipating the terrible sensation of cold metal searing into her skull. Stearne smiled.

From the thundery clouds a star fell from the storm, screeching as it tumbled from the rolling sky. In its wake a golden light drifted as it glided between the trees and towards the hunter. Stearne, distracted by the phenomenon, felt an agonising pain in his arm. A fox had lunged and clamped its jaw down, shredding the forearm with its teeth. Stearne shouted and knocked the animal away, peering at the bloodied bone and tendons exposed from the feral attack. He rose to his feet, clasping the injured arm against his chest. The star grew brighter and stronger. Ellie focused as the talons of a barn owl reached out towards her attacker.

Cyrius struck the hunter with force. Both bird and man tumbled to the ground and rolled into the trees. Talons gouged at Stearne's eyes. Streak leapt in to the melee and began savaging the throat of his victim. Feathers plumed into the air. Stearne screamed. Hopkins drew his pistol and aimed at the animals, squinting one eye as he focused on the fox. "Familiars," he whispered, taking aim.

From nowhere the weapon launched from his grasp and out into the forest. Hopkins watched as the firearm flew through the air and landed far from reach in a patch of ferns.

An eerie, dishevelled body rose ahead of him. He squinted as the wet, dirty figure of Ellie appeared. Her hair fell about her body, partly hiding her pale face. Red eyes burned through their curtains. For the first time in many years a sense of fear surged within the Witchfinder's stomach. His heart fluttered as the witch stood tall and defiant in the rain.

Ellie stared at her pursuer, her judge and executioner. The rage had now intensified to a level far above what she could comprehend. Stood silently, Ellie pointed an outstretched finger at arm's length. "You," she whispered to Hopkins, "sentenced me to death. You have killed so many of my kind and yet you yourself have been left un-judged."

Hopkins sneered. "Indeed I have, Miss Harewood. You and your kind are a threat to all mankind with your spells and practices. I have been sent by our Parliament and by God himself to rid the world of you despicable creatures." She knew by his tone that this was a false bravado.

"Then you have failed," Ellie replied, her voice now composed of more than the one in which she spoke. "You're reign of terror ends here, ends now."

Hopkins chuckled. "My dear, it is not I who reigns these lands with fear and foreboding. It is you and your kindred souls who strike terror in to the simple folk of this country."

"No! It is you, sir! What proof do you have that the people murdered by your hand were indeed practising the dark arts?" Voices of men and women long departed emerged within hers, turning her voice from a solitary entity to a chorus of sound, echoing her each and every word.

The defiant smile vanished from Hopkins face. "The truth, Miss Harewood? Is that what you seek?" He dismounted his horse and strode out to confront the witch. His cape, though soaked through with rain, billowed around him in the wind. "You want to know?" he shouted across to the harrowing figure. "You want the truth? I will speak the truth! There is no clear definition of a witch! The trials are based on very little supporting evidence! Is that what you want? We trial people purely on the basis of accusations made from their society!"

Ellie groaned and knocked Hopkins to the ground. His horse whinnied and charged away between the trees. The shrill of her scream pierced through the forest, louder and louder as Ellie continued. Her palms faced outward. She lurched forward, throwing her head to the sky as her wail grew stronger. Branches swayed above them. Leaves thundered in the wind.

Hopkins watched Ellie as she moved closer. "And what about the innocents? How many of them have you slaughtered in your quest to destroy my kind, Witchfinder?"

Hopkins expelled an amused grunt. "Too many to keep account of, Miss Harewood. I have trialled so many women and men across these lands I lose count of them. Hundreds? Thousands, maybe? But I most certainly would do so again to keep these lands safe from vermin such as you, miss. If an innocent is killed here or there, I consider it a price well paid to destroy one who worships Satan and practices witchcraft within our communities."

Ellie came to rest a few feet from the Witchfinder's place on the grass. The ground began to tremble as her mind engaged. "No more. Your murderous campaign ends here and now, and by my very hand, the hand you sought to destroy." Hopkins glared at the witch as she constricted his chest and restricted his breathing. He cast a wild, frightened glance at Ellie, seeking compassion.

"Ellie," a deep voice came to her. She found the naked human forms of Wagner and Agnieszka appear from the forest, their skin plastered with soil and blood. Their eyes remained the brilliant aura of amber unique to lycanthropes, and with the blood of enemies smeared across their faces, still looked terrifying. The werewolves joined Ellie in looking at the Witchfinder. Wagner stepped to her side. "There is no need to slaughter him. He is broken."

Ellie studied Hopkins. "Why? Why should I let him live when he has taken the lives of so many? Women. Children. Witch, warlock and wolf. Who gave him the right to become our judge and executioner?"

"None of any importance. Ellie, he is yours to do with as you wish, but consider the life he must now lead. He has no company to follow his order. The remaining survivors fled from the forest when they were left to fend on their own by this despicable leader. The hunter who took Azur from us has now been slaughtered. Azur's mother took the life and avenged her son. Your Familiars have all but crippled the man intent on causing you anguish," he explained, looking briefly at the motionless body of John Stearne.

Ellie kept her gaze upon the Witchfinder. "Your good Reverend has also perished back in Elkwood, taken directly by the hand of death himself."

"You see, then, Ellie?" Wagner said, seeking to bargain with the witch. "They are destroyed. He is destroyed. The survivors have no proof with which to prove the existence of your kind, and they will ultimately be judged by the King. Their punishment will be far worse than death, I assure you."

"And your debt to me has now been fulfilled," Samael added as he joined the creatures tormenting Hopkins. Cyrius perched on a branch hanging above his mistress. Streak appeared by her side. Both fur and feathers were tainted red.

"Consider how tormented he will be, Ellie," Wagner asked, wiping blood from his chin. "How must he feel to know that a witch of all creatures spared his life and allowed him to live? Not just to live, but to be trialled by the King, the one he sought most diligently to serve?"

Ellie grimaced. Her hands shook. Tears came from her eyes and trickled down past her trembling lips. Somewhere deep within the furthest recesses of her mind, Ellie Harewood the young woman did exist. The once compassionate, loving woman looked on Hopkins with pity. Wagner was indeed right. He was broken, and did not look any more so than he did now, saturated with rain and plastered in mud. But the compassionate Ellie Harewood soon vanished and returned the monstrous entity she had now become. Though rage flowed through her, Ellie, against her wishes, heeded the advice of her comrade. Her tearful expression turned to one of anger. "You will leave here, now, Witchfinder, and you will never return. I swear that should our paths cross again I will kill you, and of that, Master Hopkins, this time you have *my* word."

"You will fail," Hopkins began as he lurched up to his feet. He stooped, grabbed his hat, placed it on his head and wiped the dirt from his cape. "There are many more such as I roaming this world. Sooner or later you will be caught, and you will die. Not just you, Miss Harewood, all of you."

"Then that is where I will thrive. Anyone who attempts to hunt down and slaughter my allies will, in doing so, sign their own execution warrant. I have been gifted this power for a reason, and no human, town, Parliament or King will stop me. I am the harbinger of death to each and every person who opposes me." Ellie's eyes returned their natural shade. "Now leave. Face your own judge and pay the price, but do so knowing that I allowed it. I am the reason you will stand before Parliament with no evidence to present in your defence."

"Master Hopkins?" came a gurgling voice from the forest. John Stearne now stood upright. He clutched his face and throat where Ellie's Familiars had attacked. He was shredded and bloody, but alive.

Hopkins turned back to Ellie. "We will meet again, Miss Harewood, I promise you. And when we do, you would best be prepared."

"I will be waiting."

The Witchfinder General turned and strode toward his comrade. Both vanished into the trees on their way towards Elkwood. Ellie watched them disappear into the forest, struggling not to strike him down as he walked freely from the death and chaos which he had initiated.

The rain began to lighten. The force with which it struck the leaves became softer. A burden rose from Ellie's shoulders. A sense of physical release left her body. She had not saved all of Wagner's community, but many had survived. Hopkins' company had been all but destroyed. The man himself would now be summoned to Parliament to justify his actions.

Ellie looked towards her comrades and smiled. The season of the witch was upon them.

To Parliament

My Dearest Lords and Commoners,

I write this letter to you from and on behalf of the township of Elkwood , the community which I serve. This will be my last correspondence as requested on behalf of the King from this township.

We took the company of one Matthew Hopkins into our community not a fortnight ago, as our lives had become intolerable from a witch's curse. Thankfully, your esteemed selves responded to my plea of assistance and the Witchfinder arrived.

Although at times I have found his methods questionable, indeed terrifying, I am pleased to inform you that the witch has now been destroyed and our town exists peacefully once more. Unfortunately, many of my fellows lost their lives under the leadership of Master Hopkins and we are no longer a stable working community.

It is with a heavy heart that I write to inform you of our exodus from Elkwood. We are no longer at ease within the town and have decided to travel to the small village of Raunds where my good friends and colleagues have agreed to grant us citizenship. By the time you have received this letter we will have migrated already and left behind us our beloved town, abandoned within the great forest.

Master Hopkins did everything of which we asked, losing members of his own company in the process. I ask that our gratitude towards the Witchfinder be recognised and that this be taken to consideration when proceedings against his actions are debated. I am of sound mind and can vouch that had he not answered our call in our darkest of hours, the few survivors of the skirmish within the forest would not be beside us today. For that I wish to thank the Witchfinder, his company of hunters and the King for granting him permission to aid us.

My people and I now look forward to a life new and free from fear.

Your Humble Servant,

James William Randall

Horizon

"What will you do now?" Wagner asked as Ellie wrapped a shawl around her. Momentarily the memory of Luna passed through her mind, triggered by the cloak which Luna had gifted. Ellie stroked the thick garment briefly.

"I have no idea," she replied, looking at Wagner. "Find my own way in this world, I think. I will be hunted for sure, it won't stop with Hopkins. As he said, there will be many out there ready to claim the price on my head."

Agnieszka joined them. "And especially if it is discovered you are the one witch the esteemed Witchfinder could not best," she added.

Wagner placed an arm around Agnieszka's shoulder. "She is right, Ellie. The world is becoming a dangerous place for the likes of us. Why not stay here, where it is safe now from the humans?"

Ellie smiled. "It is safe, and none of you will fear changing form by the light of the moon. I, though, must start afresh. I must now find my own way in which to live. This power has changed me, and I feel I have only touched the surface of my ability. Sister Luna unlocked my mind and gave me the confidence to become the form in which I stand before you now, but for what reason? Am I here simply to protect our kind from the evils of mankind? Am I to remain dormant here until called upon? These are the questions I must have answered, and I do not believe I will find them within these trees. There has to be somebody out there. Someone must be able to help me, one way or another."

"Then please be careful, Ellie. In the world which we exist there are many negative and terrible energies that dwell. Vampires, ghosts, all of those stories are real, and they bring with them a real threat." Wagner sighed. "You must keep your wits about you. If you seek a quest of knowledge you will undoubtedly cross such people sooner or later. Remain cautious."

Ellie mused the thought for a moment. Herself, she didn't know what it was she was looking for. Maybe, deep down, she felt a sense of loyalty to Luna and those who practiced witchcraft. To honour Luna, maybe, after the sacrifices she had made to save her? All she really knew was that her time in the forest, and in Elkwood was finished. One chapter of her life had closed, but a whole new book was ready to be created.

"I doubt I will come to much harm," she replied.

"No, I do not believe you will." A moment passed between them both, a tranquil moment of peace and silence almost long since forgotten within the forest. A warm breeze rustled the leaves. Sunlight shafted down through the canopy in a golden haze. Wagner stepped towards Ellie and embraced her. A tear came to her eye. "No matter what, no matter where, if you need me, call to me," he whispered, placing a hand on her soft hair. "I will come to you, through Hell and high water if need be." Ellie looked up at him and nodded. "And you two, look after her," he said over Ellie's shoulder. Cyrius bobbed his head and Streak barked in response.

"Do not worry, Wagner. I can take care of myself," she laughed, wiping a tear from her cheek.

"So I have witnessed."

Ellie left his embrace and turned to the vast forest into which she was about to venture. As she wandered away she turned round one last time. Agnieszka waved. Ellie smiled. "Remember, Ellie. Just call," Wagner shouted. Ellie tapped her finger twice on her temple and turned away.

Cyrius swooped from the canopy and hovered above his mistress, tracking her progress. Streak bounded along beside her. "Do you think we will see her again?" Agnieszka asked, as the grey shawl disappeared between the trees.

185

"I believe so, Agnieszka, I believe so. She feels there is much to do now that her power has been realised, and who are we to argue? Ellie must decide her own fate from here on, and I don't believe this is the last we will see of her."

Epilogue

Fire burned intensely on top of the wind-swept hill. A large coven gathered in the cold air as the wind blasted between them and around their Sabbath. Many of the witches were old and haggard, much like their local community had come to recognise and fear. Some were young and new to the terrifying practices of the Dark Lord. The body of an infant boy lay lifeless and drained, sacrificed in response to a request from the demon that towered before them. A sense of awe gripped the coven as the beast glared at their tattered shawls and simple, cotton dresses.

Ascending the incline a warlock approached. Across his shoulders swayed a large sack, bound tightly in twine and soiled with earth.

"What kept you?" a timeworn witch snapped as she shuffled toward the advancing man. The demon took notice as the warlock moved towards the fire.

"It wasn't us, it was the horses! They wouldn't venture any closer! We had to carry them from the bottom!"

"Idiots!" the woman sighed, turning her attention to the man who followed, carrying a similar burden.

The two sacks thudded to the ground beside the fire. The demon studied them from top to bottom. "And you are sure?" its deep voice asked.

"Indeed, yes. They were exactly where you told us we should dig," the warlock replied. The demon leaned over, its broken horns only now beginning to re-emerge.

"What does our Dark Lord require us to do with these?" the wrinkled woman asked as she stared at the bound bundles.

"It is not the Dark Lord's bidding, it is mine," the beast replied. "Upon this plain his power is reduced and realised through the servants of the dark arts. Worshippers such as this coven fulfil his bidding and create the fear on which he thrives. However, one such entity walks amongst you with a free will, and power far greater than he has ever imagined for a mere mortal. I will deliver her soul to him personally, before she becomes too vengeful."

"Why then have we delivered these bodies to you?" the hag enquired, looking to the bundles that rested at her feet. "If this entity of which you speak is so powerful, surely there is nothing that we can do to thwart it?"

"Exactly," the demon growled, "nothing *you* can do."

The bound material burst into flame, frightening the witch. She stumbled backwards away from the fires. The bundles shook and twisted. Gurgles and groans emanated from within. The warlock took hold of the hag and pulled her back into the coven. Skeletons emerged from the amber light, shaking and twisting in the flames. Muscle and sinew crept over their bones, oozing blood as they bonded to the frame. Eyes appeared in the skulls. Screams echoed across the hill as muscle and ligament appeared on their throats, displaying the agony of their reincarnation. Hair sprouted from the forming flesh. Skin grew over muscle. Finally the contorted forms of two women slumped to their knees in front of the demon, their bodies glistening with sweat in the flame's light.

The beast roared. "Who is the one whom you serve?" it asked, peering down on the naked pair. One woman looked upward. Her body trembled. "The Dark Lord," she gasped.

"The Dark Lord," the other repeated.

"And who are you? Why have I been gracious enough to resurrect you from the Hell in which you were spawned? Tell me your names!"

The women shivered.

"Demdike," one replied. A murmur came from the terrified coven.

"Chattox," whispered the other.

188

The coven erupted in hysteria. Witches and warlocks ran from the hill, screaming and wailing as they sprinted from the Sabbath and into the darkness.

"Silence," the demon bellowed. Order restored amongst those brave enough to remain. "Now, explain to me who you were remembered as, in life. By what notoriety were you known throughout these lands? Tell me!"

Demdike looked toward her master. A brief expression of malevolence appeared on her face. "In life, we were the leaders of a coven known as the Pendle Witches."

The demon stooped low and smiled. "Indeed you were, and the most powerful of your kind to exist within this world."

"None dared to question us. None dared to challenge us. The entire county lived in fear during our practice," Chattox added, warming herself by the fire. "Together we were the most powerful of our kind."

"And indeed you will be once more, witches. I will grant that you keep your lives in return for one simple request."

"What is it that you ask of us, my lord?" Chattox asked the creature as it stood proudly within the fire's flames.

"I ask nothing more than a simple exchange. Your lives for another. A witch walks across this earth, more powerful than any to set foot on this plain." The demon grazed across the scars to its abdomen lightly, recalling the one who had bested it in battle. "I want her destroyed, and her soul delivered to my domain. You are the last witches in history who can mirror her power, together, not alone. I want you to find her. I want you to destroy her. Deliver her body to me and you will be granted an extension of your natural life, and be free to wreak Satan's work upon this world once again. Do we agree?"

The Pendle witches bathed in the pagan fire which imprisoned the demon. Away in the distance thunder clapped and rolled as it approached Pendle Hill. Its two most notorious witches, now resurrected from the dead, walked the earth once more. The demon awaited the witches' answer. Demdike and Chattox looked at each other before bursting in to cackle that chilled the coven to their core.

Made in the USA
Charleston, SC
25 April 2016